Dangerous Occupation

Doris Holland

AuthorHouse™
1663 Liberty Drive
Bloomington, IN 47403
www.authorhouse.com
Phone: 1-800-839-8640

© 2010 Doris Holland. All rights reserved.

No part of this book may be reproduced, stored in a retrieval system, or transmitted by any means without the written permission of the author.

First published by AuthorHouse 12/21/2010

ISBN: 978-1-4520-9461-8 (e)
ISBN: 978-1-4520-9460-1 (dj)
ISBN: 978-1-4520-9459-5 (sc)

Library of Congress Control Number: 2010918469

Printed in the United States of America

This book is printed on acid-free paper.

Certain stock imagery © Thinkstock.

Because of the dynamic nature of the Internet, any Web addresses or links contained in this book may have changed since publication and may no longer be valid. The views expressed in this work are solely those of the author and do not necessarily reflect the views of the publisher, and the publisher hereby disclaims any responsibility for them.

Prologue

"Mrs. Martin, ah, I see you are coming around now. Can you hear me? I'm Nurse Grace. You can just call me Gracie."

The nurse was talking to Lydia in her nurturing voice as she continued to check the tubes which were connected to her patient. "You're in the hospital. Now don't you worry. We'll take good care of you here at Mercy. I'm just going to take your temp and blood pressure. Dr. Matthews will be coming in soon." When she finished noting the list of vitals, she replaced the chart and continued to talk to Lydia.

Lydia could hear the woman in the multiple colored smock. But she seemed to be talking through a tunnel and kept going in and out of focus.

"What's wrong with me? Where did she say I am? In the hospital? Why? God my head is throbbing so. What happened?"

"Mrs. Martin, Dr. Matthews wants me to get you up as soon as I can. It's not good to stay in bed too long. I'm going to get your bath ready. I just know we'll want to freshen up after being asleep such a long time. I am so glad you finally woke up. You had us worried there for awhile. It has been 2 weeks since they brought you in. Since it has been so long since you have been on your feet I will help steady you. "

The bright light of the room made Lydia squint as she tried to focus. It was pleasantly furnished with a wooden dresser made of cherry with a mirror to match. There was a brass floor lamp which was placed behind the bed. The privacy curtain was decorated with purple and green tulips and tied back with a purple sash.

My mouth is so dry I could spit dust. And it tastes like a herd of goats just tromped through. Every heartbeat makes my head feel like an explosion. Did she say I was in the hospital? Why am I here? Oh my Lord Jesus what has happened to me? Why is my mind failing me?

Gracie spoke gently reminding her again that she was getting the shower ready. "Wouldn't you like take a shower? It may help to clear your head."

"Yes, I would like a shower and brush this grime off my teeth." Lydia responded with voice that sounded strange to her. *"Did I say that or did I just think it? My head hurts so badly I can't tell."*

"OK, Mrs. Martin. But we will have to take it easy. We'll just sit up first. And when our head stops spinning, we'll try to stand up on our feet."

What's all this "we" stuff? I don't see anyone else with her. Oh well, she is kind enough to help me so I shouldn't mention that to her. Anyway, she looks strong enough to carry me to the bath and kick my butt as well for correcting her English. So I think I'll just keep that to myself.

The shower did make her feel better. But it took a while to get the cotton taste out of her mouth. As she stepped out of the shower with the help of Gracie, Lydia's loose towel slipped off her at the same time Dr Matthews knocked and entered the room.

"My patients are usually lying down when I examine them", he smiled with a twinkle in his eyes. He picked up the towel and wrapped it around Lydia and helped her get into bed.

"Can you beat that?" thought Gracie. What happened to the starch he usually has in his bedside manner? He must be trying to smooth things a bit to make it a little easier for what she is about to face."

Dr. Matthews examined Lydia, made a few notes, and frowned as he gave Gracie a few instructions about meds and therapy.

Why the frown? Is there something seriously wrong with me other that this terrific headache?

"By the way, let's just keep the missing towel incident to ourselves. Leroy may not think it was funny."

This made her remember that she had duties back at home and Leroy didn't like for her to be gone for long. "When do you think I will be able to go home?" asked Lydia.

Dr. Matthews glanced at Gracie then back to Lydia, "It may a few days. You just focus on getting better by exercising to get your strength back. I have set up therapy sessions for you for a week." He motioned for Gracie to follow him out.

When the door opened for them to leave Lydia caught a glimpse of a uniformed guard in the hall.

"Now may be the time to let Mrs. Martin know that her husband is dead. It would be better coming from you than from the deputy here. I guess we'd better call the sheriff, too, since he informed me that he was to be called ASAP when she woke up."

Chapter 1

Leroy, as usual on Tuesday, headed out to meet Rev. Bradley Goodman at 8:30 for breakfast. He stopped at Beulah Land Church to pick up the Preacher. There was another man with Rev. Goodman when he entered the church office; Bradley introduced him to Phillip Williams. "Phillip just moved here to head up an insurance branch in this area. He was just telling me that he is looking for a church. Why don't you show him around while I finish up here? I'll be right back. It won't take me long."

Leroy offered his hand which was received with a firm handshake. *"Feels like a salesman's shake,"* thought Leroy as he assured him that everyone was welcome. "As the head of the New Members Committee, I will be happy to answer any questions you may have." The two chatted as they toured the various rooms in the building and returned to the office where Rev. was slipping into a jacket.

"Say, if you have the time why don't you join us for breakfast at Matty's Diner?" Rev. Goodman asked as he held the door for them, "It's just across the street."

"Thanks, I've already had breakfast, but I would like a second cup of coffee" answered Phillip as they headed out.

The 3 men entered and were greeted with the same salutation as every Tuesday…

"Morning boys. The usual?" Matty gave them her cherry smile. Matty always greeted everyone with her "glad to see you" smile. Her saying was, "You can't give away a smile because it is always returned"

"Yep", was the reply from the two regulars. "Just coffee for me, thanks," Phillip offered.

Matty served up "The usual" for Leroy: a slice of country ham, two eggs, biscuit, gravy and coffee. "This sure beats what I had at home", Leroy said as he spooned the gravy over the biscuit. *He says this every Tuesday. I know Lydia is a good cook. I don't know why he has to put her down so*", Matty thought but smiled at him anyway. *"I guess there's no changing the old goat".* Matty gave him this secret title because of the tuft of hair that he called a mustache growing on his chin.

The other two men made no comment. Rev. Goodman had toast, eggs, and coffee. Phillip was served coffee.

"Well, the gang's all here," laughed Matty when Sophie and Alice came in. The two women had just happened to come at the same time for a bite before heading to work. Sophie, a real estate broker stopped in whenever she had a showing in the area. Alice ran a beauty shop two blocks down.

"Why don't you two share a booth and save room for my other customers?" Matty giggled as she waved her wet dish cloth at the empty booths. Most of her customers came early around 6 AM and this was a lull between breakfast and lunch. Matty usually let her help take a break during the lull so she was the cook and waitress at this time.

Phillip looked around at the cherry diner. It was circular in shape and 8 tables were placed in a half moon position in front of the stainless steel kitchen and serving area. Matty liked the open atmosphere where conversation between customers was the norm.

Soft yellow plastic cloths covered the tables. The walls were painted with a light pastel color which had hint of pea green. Mark, Matty's husband, had painted a row of barnyard cartoon characters marching around the top of the wall. They each held a kitchen tool as if playing a musical instrument as they marched.

Mark, a quiet person had a great sense of humor. He would help Matty out when there was a rush of customers. But he preferred to be out taking pictures of unusual subjects. He freelanced for the local paper and wrote interesting stories about his finds. Every so often one of his pieces would make it to national news.

Matty loved both being around people and cooking. So this was the ideal profession for her. She said it also gave her an excuse to be nosey.

Sophie and Alice spoke as they passed. The three men nodded. Leroy made the comment that Alice sure was a pretty woman. Phillip wondered what was under those layers of makeup but kept it to himself since he was the newcomer.

Sophie was served a poached egg, whole wheat toast and black coffee. Sophie worked out at the gym to keep her sturdy frame in check. Alice, on the other hand, had no trouble with her weight. She had a hardy appetite and had ordered bacon, eggs, a waffle with plenty of butter and coffee with half and half.

"Nothing sticks to your bones, does it Alice?" laughed Matty. It made her day when her customers enjoyed the food she prepared. It just got to her when Leroy made degrading remarks about his wife. *"He may think it is funny but I just don't find it funny to belittle another".*

Leroy insisted on paying the bill and left a generous tip. They walked out, Rev. Goodman and Phillip headed to their respective offices and Leroy to the farm.

A few days later Leroy called Phillip to ask him to come over to discuss insurance. Leroy answered the knock at the door. "Phillip, come on in. Thanks for coming on short notice. I need to get this over with and get to the bank. I was just there for a loan and they tried to sell me some of their insurance. I just didn't like what they had. But I feel that I need to upgrade what I do have. That's when I remembered that you were into insurance."

"Well, let's see if we can set you up with just what you need" Phillip said as he opened his briefcase, and set out several pamphlets. "How much insurance do you have now? We may be able to save money by consolidating. I noticed that you have two trucks and some farm machinery. Did you know that farming is the most dangerous occupation when it comes to accidents and death?"

"Why yes, I was just saw that on the news. That's why I decided to check my policies. I can see where that could be true what with having to repair our own farm machinery and the chemicals we have to use.

"And we can't discount the wife's cooking" he laughed. "Of course that may be the other part of the report which said that the home was where accidents happen most often."

Leroy looked at several options and explained, "I don't usually insure all of my machinery. But I heard that there have been several break-ins around lately. Also some large equipment has been stolen from construction sites in the lower part of the state. There's no telling when they might move up here. Since I just purchased a new tractor and equipment I need to protect my investment. It would cost a pretty penny to replace the farm equipment if something should happen. Also the Farm Bureau suggested that I make sure the farm is insured in case someone gets hurt on the farm.

"I may be able to save you some money if you want to group several policies together."

"OK, now I think I have a handle on what you want. This is the list so far: double indemnity accidental dismemberment or death, farm liability, home, and Farm machinery including the trucks and your wife's auto. What I need now is the information on the farm equipment and vehicles, and we should be finished. I'll just get this typed up and bring the papers back for you to sign.

Phillip stacked up the papers and slid them into the briefcase, shook Leroy's hand and promised to return as soon as he had finished the paperwork.

The next Tuesday Phillip brought the policy to be signed. Leroy was annoyed, "I am sorry I need to leave shortly. You must have forgotten that I always have breakfast with The Reverend on Tuesday. I do need to get this over with so let me read it. I don't sign anything unless I read it first. You put everything in that we discussed, I see. Leroy scanned the policy but pretended to speed read it. Then he signed in all the appropriate places.

Phillip gave Leroy his copy and declined the invitation to join the two friends for breakfast. Even though it was too early for his office to be open, he said that he had other business he needed to do. He couldn't put his finger on it but there was something about the Good Reverend and Leroy that just didn't set right with him. It was as if they had the answer to all the world's problems. Anyone who disagreed with them was naïve, lacking in the mental department, or had no idea how to solve problems.

Chapter 2

PHILLIP KNOCKED ON THE MARTIN'S door. Leroy had asked him to stop by because he had bought another piece of farm equipment and wanted to go over the policy to see if everything was in order. He was also worried about the recent break-ins that had been happening in the area. Even though Phillip told him he did not have much time to talk Leroy had insisted that he come by.

He had told Leroy that he couldn't take long because he will be on the way to the airport. "I'm in a hurry because the regional manager has suffered a heart attack and I have to go to the home office to take over."

"You should know that farming is the most dangerous occupation there is. So I want to make sure my all my equipment is covered in case I am hurt in an accident." Leroy insisted in a demanding tone. "Are you or are you not my insurance agent?"

"Yes, I am but not for long. My replacement will be here as soon as one is found and travel arrangements are made. You don't have to worry about it though. Just call the main office if you need anything until then. You should have the number with the policy.

"He seems to be in such a tizzy I guess I'd better placate him," thought Phillip as he threw his suitcase in the trunk. His other things were left for his replacement to pack and ship. "I'd better leave now. By the tone of his voice it may take awhile. AND I don't have much time."

There was no answer to his knock.

"That's strange Leroy insisted that I come right over. He sounded impatient and said that he would be waiting."

As he looked around he saw Leroy's truck was parked in the yard. When He looked in the window of the garage he saw that Lydia's car was there. So there was no indication that either Leroy or Lydia was out.

Phillip went to the kitchen door and peered in to see if he could see anyone as he knocked and called out. When there was no answer he tried the door. It was unlocked so he walked in again calling out to Leroy and Lydia. Leroy had told him that sometimes he was working in the back and did not always hear when people came.

"Hello, Leroy, it's Phillip. Are you here?"

That is when he saw the reason no one answered. Leroy was lying on the floor in a pool of blood. As he rushed about frantically in search for the phone he found Lydia just at the corner in the hall. She too was lying on the floor. There was a pool of blood at her head. He called 911 and explained the situation. The operator told him to stay on the line and asked about the extent of injuries. He explained to her that he could not find a pulse when he checked Leroy. But there was a faint heart beat from Lydia. He told the operator that he could not revive either of the Martins. He assured the operator that he would wait until someone came but he had only a few minutes because it was imperative that he leave as soon as they got there because he had to catch his flight to Chicago. Then realized he was babbling, giving the operator more information than she wanted.

Being quite shook up and not knowing many people in the community, Phillip called Rev. Goodman and told him what he had found.

"Lord have mercy. I know you must be in shock to find them as you did. Now don't you worry about a thing. I'll be right over."

As soon as he hung up the phone Rev. Goodman called the co-presidents of the Members Care Committee to let them know that there may be a need for their services at the Martin home. Twins, Essie and Bessie, Cindy Lou, Amy, Henryetta, and Marlene volunteered for the position because they were homemakers and such good friends. Besides that, they let the church members know that they met each morning for a "Munch & Chat" session. So, as they were noted to say, "It only follows that we are best suited for taking care of those less fortunate".

DANGEROUS OCCUPATION

Now, the members of this committee take this roll very seriously. And they let no moss grow under their feet. They were not at all shy when there was such a good chance of being the first to learn about a juicy story. Not that they were gossips, mind you, just concerned citizens. So by the time the good reverend headed out his door, all 6 members had been notified and were making a beeline to the Martin House.

When Rev. Goodman arrived he assured Phillip that there was no need for him to miss his flight because he would wait for EMS.

"There is nothing you can do for poor Leroy and the ladies will take care of Lydia. So you go on and don't give it a second thought."

Even though he had promised to stay, Leroy reluctantly agreed to leave because there was nothing else he could do.

"I never cared much for Leroy, but I hate that this happened to him. I don't even care much for the good reverend and I hate to leave Lydia in the hands of the ladies who loved to "spread the word" at the Alice's beauty shop. But I just can't miss that flight," thought Phillip as he left wishing there was something else he could do.

When the paramedics arrived they found the group in different sections of the large room. They had to shoulder their way to Leroy. Henryetta was wringing her hands mumbling, "Lordy, Lordy" over Leroy as Rev. Goodman was reciting a long mournful prayer.

Exasperated and nervous the twins tried to tend to Lydia. Skinny as a pole Essie and Bessie with great effort had lifted Lydia off the floor and lay her on the sofa.

They were so shaken they spoke in endless chatter, "She won't stay on the couch. She keeps sliding off to the floor." "I think she is trying to wake up. What should we do? Do you think we should put a cold pack on the bump on her head?"

"I think the blood on her head needs to be cleaned off first." Cindy Lou offered as she headed to the kitchen.

It had taken all the energy Marlene had to waddle over on her short legs to the recliner, where she sat down huffing and puffing and leaned the recliner back as far as it would go. There she sat fanning herself with her feet up in the air, "My goodness, me I just might faint right here. Do boys think I may pass out?"

Marlene did love her sweets and could really pack away the morning munches. Amy, who warned her about her weight, said, "Essie plus Bessie makes one Marlene"

Amy, ever the industrious one, had righted the pink glider that had overturned and returned the brass table lamp she found in the corner back to Leroy's reading table. She did not notice the small splotch of blood on it. "Boy this little lamp sure is heavy for its size. It must have rolled over there when it fell."

The paramedics first checked Leroy. Finding him dead, they then went to Lydia and were placing her on the stretcher when the Sheriff Chester McCormick showed up with the coroner."

"What in the world is going on here? This is no place for you women to be", Boomed Sheriff McCormick.

With this proclamation, everything came to a screeching halt. Marlene whose feet were skyward brought the recliner down with a crash, Essie and Bessie stopped trying to prop up Lydia, Amy held onto a boot which she had just picked up from the floor, Rev. Goodman ceased praying in mid sentence, and Henryetta started wringing her hands even more frantically.

"There are entirely too many people in here. I can't possibly make head or tails of this with you milling around. Go home! Stay there until I can get back with you! And don't say a word about this until I have a look at things here. You will have to tell me everything you did before I came."

"Come on girls, let's go to my house and get out of the sheriff's way and let him do his job. We'll be at my house Sheriff when you need to talk." Amy said as she ushered them out looking back over her shoulder. She was looking at the sheriff with a forced smile and ran right into the Deputy Crane as he rushed in.

"Sheriff, do you think this could be connected to robberies we've been having lately?" Deputy Douglas Crane asked out of breath.

He quickly closed his mouth when Sheriff McCormick frowned at him."Don't jump to any conclusions until we check the place out. Besides I don't see anything worth stealing. Do you? Who would want a collection of old farm tools?"

Searching the room turned up a knob in the corner, "Looks like it may have come from a lamp." Deputy Crane mumbled to himself as he placed it into an evidence bag.

DANGEROUS OCCUPATION

As the sheriff and deputy checked the room they found blood in several places. They had put on plastic gloves to make sure their finger prints were not left on anything. "There has been enough contamination done already." Sheriff McCormick grumbled as he glared at the surroundings. Since the women had replaced some items there was no way for them to know where everything had been or whose fingerprints would be on them.

There was blood splattered on most of the furniture and wall beyond where Leroy was found. There was blood on the sofa where Lydia had been, on the scales and weights, the rocker, the anvil, and lamp. As he picked up the cotton scales Sheriff McCormick thought that there was more than one item that may have been the murder weapon. *"Any one of these old farm tools could have been used. Each of Leroy's collection of mementoes certainly was heavy enough."*

"Douglas, get a forensic over here to get fingerprints. There's no telling how many will be found with all the people who have been in here. I know they mean well, but darn it, things like this make my job so much harder."

The sheriff jotted down notes: "Lydia found on couch, Leroy nearby on floor, cotton scales on floor near the wall, blood on brass lamp on side table. Nuts, bolts, odds and ends on floor, looks as if Leroy emptied his pockets on table and it was turned over. None of the other room were disturbed. Nothing seems to be missing. No evidence of anyone searching for something. Could be attempted murder suicide. Need more information."

The sheriff was no closer to answers after he talked with the women who were frantic. They had overheard Deputy Crane's comment about the break-ins and were chattering about how unsafe the neighborhood was getting."This used to be such a nice safe place to bring up children. Why, we never even locked our doors at night it was so safe. Now look what's happened. I just know I'll not be able to sleep a wink at night." Whined Henryetta.

"Okay ladies," Sheriff McCormick tried to stay calm "I'm sorry I was a little harsh with you before. I was just reacting to what I saw. I know you are quite upset that's only natural from what you just experienced. But I want you to stop a minute and take a few breaths to settle your nerves. Amy, do you think you could made cup of tea for us?"

After the tea, Sheriff McCormick thought he could now get a few lucid answers to his questions. "Now I know you ladies were trying to help. You are always willing to give help where it is needed. But I need for you to try to think clearly and just tell me what you saw and what you did." The sheriff had learned from years of experience that sometimes a pat on the back got more answers than a threat.

When they all started to talk at once, Sheriff McCormick wiped his large hand down his face and pasted on a smile. "Why don't I just ask one of you at a time? Amy you go first."

"When I got there I saw Lydia and Leroy on the floor. There was lots of blood around Leroy's head. I know how Lydia likes a neat house so I picked up a few things. Let me think. I picked up the rocker. Oh yes, I found a lamp in the corner. So I put it back on the table. That's about it."

"Henryetta?"

"I didn't do much I just saw poor Leroy lying there on the floor dead."

"Cindy Lou?"

"As Amy said Lydia liked to be neat. I saw the blood on her head so I got a cloth from the kitchen to wipe it off. That's all I did."

"Marlene?"

"I nearly passed out from all that blood. I was so weak had to sit down. So I sat down in the recliner and leaned back to clear my head."

"Essie, Bessie you're last."

Essie had her hand over her mouth about to cry as Bessie answered. "Since Leroy was dead we tried to revive Lydia. We were trying to get her on the sofa but she kept sliding off. That's when you came in Sheriff."

Chapter 3

Lydia looked up as a man in a freshly pressed military creased khaki uniform walked in. He was robust and stood straight and tall. It appeared that he had been through some type of in military training.

"Mrs. Martin," his voice filled the room. "I'm Sheriff Chester McCormick. Most people just call me Sheriff. I'll just get right to the reason I am here. I know this must seem to be bad timing on my part but I'm investigating your husband's death. Too much time has passed already. We have been waiting for two weeks for you to wake up." He did not offer his hand when he introduced himself and his face was emotionless.

Nurse Grace had told her about Leroy's death just before the sheriff came in. Lydia had seen a deputy standing outside her hospital and asked about it.

Dr. Matthews had told Grace "Now may be the time to tell Mrs. Martin that her husband is dead. It would better coming from you than from the deputy here. The sheriff informed me that he was to be called ASAP when she woke up."

"I have been told that you had a concussion and may have trouble remembering but there are a few things that we need to ask you. It's unclear as to what happened to you and Leroy. It is so confusing and no one seems to be able to explain what happened."

The sheriff shifted his position and looked at Nurse Grace. His composure changed to one of indecision. "Miss Grace, This may take awhile you may to want to leave."

Since she had been by Lydia's nurse for two weeks she felt like a mother hen protecting her brood, "I'll stay if you she wants me. AND the doctor said she needs to rest and you shouldn't stay long."

"Please stay", pleaded Lydia.

"If that is what you want."

"I'm confused myself. Nurse Grace just told me that Leroy was dead. How did he die? What happened? Ohhh, I have such a terrific headache and my head is spinning so it is hard for me to think straight.

"That's what I'm saying," Mrs. Martin. We don't know what happened and I am trying to get to the bottom of it. That's why I must ask you to stay available. After you leave the hospital you are to stay in this area. You are not to go out of the state until this has been cleared up. Do you understand what I am saying?"

"This is so confusing. Why would I leave? I have no plans to go anywhere I'm here in a hospital. Have I done something wrong that would cause you to suggest that I stay in the area?"

Sheriff McCormick looked down at his shoes and hesitated for a minute and shook his head. Then he looked at Lydia with a serious frown, "Let's just say I want to be able to get in contact with you if I have any more questions.

"Everything is fuzzy. Do we have to talk right now? Can't we do this tomorrow?"

Sheriff McCormick shook his head, "I'm afraid I can't wait another day. I need to clear this up while it is still fresh in your mind. I don't want anything to get in the way of the truth. Sometimes other problems tend to cloud the memory. Besides the Doctor said that you may be able to go home soon and I can't let you go without getting your statement. Otherwise I will have to send a police escort with you to insure that you won't escape, I mean, leave before we have a chance to find out just what happened." He said this with a hint of a smile.

Sheriff McCormick took out a tape recorder and pulled a chair close to the bed, "I will be recording this interview so there will be no question as to what you or I said."

DANGEROUS OCCUPATION

The sheriff sat down in the chair and turned on the recorder. "Now tell me what happened on June 28th of this year? That's the day Leroy died"

Lydia frowned as she tried to think back to that day. Her head still ached and trying to remember made it worse. It felt like a balloon was pressing on her brain.

"I don't remember what day it was. I'll just try to remember the last things that happened before Nurse Grace spoke to me here in the hospital. I remember fixing dinner. Leroy was taking off his boots as he usually does when he comes in to eat. We sat down… No, wait we didn't sit down. I had to go to the bathroom. That's all I remember. I don't remember anything after that."

"Try Mrs. Martin. What did you do after you came back from the bathroom?"

"I'm trying Sheriff. It's just a blank." Lydia said weakly as she sank down further on the bed and her eyes rolled back in her head.

"That's enough, Sheriff!" Grace had her hands on her hips. "I don't want her to slip back into a coma."

He sat back and waited while Grace glared at him. "If she comes back around I want to ask just one more question. Let me try. Mrs. Martin?"

Lydia's eyes fluttered and finally opened.

'Mrs. Martin what time was this? What time was dinner?"

"Dinner? We always ate at noon." Lydia slowly answered with her eyes closed.

"Mrs. Martin…"

"Sheriff!" interrupted the nurse. "You have had your **one question.** You have to leave now."

"Okay, okay I'll be back tomorrow."

It was late in the afternoon when Lydia woke up as Grace slipped in to check on her. "Well now do we feel better? You do seem to have better color in your face. You have had a lot of company while you were out. I'm sure there will be friends coming by tomorrow. So get some sleep. Goodnight.

Chapter 4

LYDIA WAS ONLY 6 MONTHS old when her mother died. Aunt Ruth wrapped the child up in a blanket and carried her back home with her and there she stayed. Lydia didn't know much about her father. He was seldom mentioned. It seems that he was so heartbroken he left town and no one heard from him after that. Aunt Ruth's motto was, "We accept God's blessings and endure the trials." She considered Lydia one of God's blessings.

After graduating from high school Lydia went to community college and earned a degree in accounting. After that she earned a mechanical engineering degree and another in interior design. But because she wanted to be near her Aunt Ruth who was getting on in years she continued to work at the neighborhood pharmacy. She had started working for Bob Partain on weekends when she was 16. "This will get you out of my hair", teased Aunt Ruth."

After graduating Aunt Ruth encouraged Lydia to get a job in a larger city, but neither of them could find a suitable solution. Mr. Partain gave her free reign in designing and setting up window designs. She was her own boss and that left time to take short trips with Ruth whenever the notion struck. Later there were plenty of offers to practice her skills in other places of businesses. She walked to work most days because she loved to be outside and it was only 5 blocks away. So the two of them just grew into a settled and contented lifestyle.

On Saturday afternoons Leroy came by to take Lydia to the early movie. He worked on the family farm ten miles away. Kate, Lydia's friend from high school had introduced them. Kate had been dating Leroy's cousin at the time. They double dated some until Kate started seeing another boy. She didn't like to go out that early and liked to stay out later. Leroy said he needed to get home early and get to bed because he was expected to be up at five in the morning. So the two close friends grew apart. They still were best friends. They were just no longer together every waking moment.

"Now wasn't that an inspiring message today?" mused Ruth as they sat on the porch. They had just finished Sunday dinner. "We know that we are all sinners but the preacher doesn't leave us there in condemnation. He lifts us up with hope with the reminder that God sent his son with loving forgiveness. Jesus was sent as the Sacrificial Lamb so that we have reason to be happy and enjoy life. When I leave church I leave with an uplifted spirit."

They looked out at the small town they called home. As they sat there they started walking down memory lane. They both loved where they lived and would not dream of living anywhere else. It had been home to them all their lives.

The small historic town of Windfield grew around the old farmers market. This was the central place where farmers brought their grain and other goods to be shipped by rail to cities across the country. After railroads were no longer used as the main mode of transportation for these goods, the town just stopped growing. It was a typical small town. In the middle of the square sat the courthouse. Shops of various kinds lined the each side of the squares. Even though the buildings showed the effects of old age and was in need of a face lift, it was kept clean and neat by the merchants who were proud of their town.

Chapter 5

Lydia was busy in the pharmacy window changing the display. Since Mr. Partain gave her free reign on this, she was enjoying herself as she set up the model train with Santa and his elves. The track took up most of the window. As the train circled around the track, Santa and his elves loaded the cars with small packages wrapped with colorful Christmas paper and red and green ribbon. She had taken great pains in the planning. She made use of her degree in mechanical engineering degree as well as the degree in home decorating and design. It took a lot of time to set the timing it so that the mobile Santa would reach just the right spot to load packages and the elves at the end to be in the exact place to unload them. A conveyor belt was placed behind a Christmas tree. That was where the packages were recycled to make the trip around again. This kept the loop going. The Christmas tree was decorated with items that pharmacy had on special sale for the holidays.

Lydia looked up to see the White family watching her as she worked. As she waved at them she wondered what this Christmas would hold for them. Because of an accident Jules White was still in the hospital and thus not able to work. His wife, Jan had her hands full caring for their three small children. Lydia knew there would be little for them at Christmas. Her aunt Ruth had been busy deciding what to get them for Christmas and how to get it to them without hurting their pride.

DANGEROUS OCCUPATION

Aunt Ruth arranged for their pastor to get a delivery truck to deliver the items which included toys and clothes for each child. These were stored in a large box with a letter of instructions to the parents. They were to open the box without the children there. This would allow the parents to have something from Santa. In fact the letter was signed Santa. There was also a Christmas turkey with all the trimmings ready to be cooked on Christmas day. The driver of the truck and his helper could not tell where the goods came from because they did not know. It was arranged through a third party. Aunt Ruth had gone through several sources so that it would be hard to trace. She really enjoyed doing this. She just loved being the instigator of a mystery.

The next week as Lydia was working on the beauty shop display Missy Gordon came by to watch. She seemed so excited with a wide grin on her face. Missy, usually a very shy 13 year old, lived with her sister's family, the White's. Lydia motioned for her to come around where she was.

Lydia chatted with Missy as she worked. "You sure look happy today. What's going on?"

"The most wonderful thing happened. I prayed so hard for God to help Jan's babies to have a happy Christmas. I wanted to get a job or stay with the children so that Jan could get a job. But nothing came our way. Jan told me to stop worrying that God would take care of us. Christmas may be slim but that's all right, we have each other. And even though he may be crippled Jules is alive. So at our Thanksgiving meal Jan asked each to tell what we had to be thankful for."

Missy giggled as she told that 5 year old Jay was thankful for the soup "even though it didn't have much meat in it"

"But that's not the best part". Missy went on, "There was a big box brought to our door and Jan said that a guardian angel had sent it for Christmas and for me to wipe that worry right off my face." She would not show what was in the box except for a big turkey packed in ice, pumpkin pie, and lots of other goodies."

The smile slipped a little. She dropped her head as she went on, "I heard Jan talking with Jules about it and they were trying to guess who sent it and how they were to pay it back"

Lydia took Missy's chin in her hand and raised her head it to meet her eyes," Just where did that big grin go? Put it right back. Unless I am totally wrong, everyone who has seen your bright smile today has enjoyed that gift as much as your family. Your sister is right. God heard your prayers and sent an angel your way and He wants you to accept the blessing. Some day you may be able to send a blessing to another. That would be payment enough, don't you think?"

Melissa nodded with a smile and turned her attention to the display. Lydia had replaced the Thanksgiving theme with a Christmas one. It didn't take much because it was a simple scene with a family around a table. Each season or holiday Lydia had planned to change it to fit the occasion. Off to the side were Christmas wrappings and small boxes to be wrapped as gifts as if the family stopped their work to sit down to eat.

"Miss Lydia, how did you learn to do this?" Melissa asked as she surveyed the moving heads and arms of the dolls as they appeared to be eating. Well, I have always liked to see what made things work. Aunt Ruth said that if she left me alone long enough her entire house would be laid out in little pieces where I took them apart. That is the reason I went to community college to study mechanical engineering as well as interior decorating and design. Just then Jan appeared at the window and waved.

"I have to run Sis must be finished with her shopping. Thanks for showing me your window designs". Melissa left with the wide smile still on her face. Lydia too was smiling as she thought how good it was to have this smart young girl to stop in to see her.

When her work in this window was finished Lydia headed home with a happy smile on her face. As she walked home she prayed, "Thank you God for giving me this talent. I just love to design these displays. It also lets me bring joy to others as well.

It had taken Lydia 2 months to finish the windows for both businesses. She did not take pay for the Christmas scenes. "This is my Christmas gift to the town." She always replied when they tried to pay her.

The next day as she went to work at the pharmacy she noticed a crowd around the window. They were laughing at something. When she pushed through she started laughing with them. The train had derailed and packages were piled on the rail tracks. Santa had tipped over on his side and was going round and round, his arms waving in the air.

"Well the batteries are still working", laughed Lydia. "I'm glad the safety switch worked. It cut off the electricity to the track. Oh well as the saying goes Rome wasn't built in a day. I'll have to do some repair work and redo my plans on Mr. Santa"

"Hey," came a male voice from the crowd. "Leave it that way. I like it." This brought more laughter as the crowd thinned out and moved on.

Chapter 6

LYDIA'S AUNT RUTH DIED QUIETLY in her sleep May 15, at the age of 97. Just the day before, as Lydia dressed for work at Partain's Pharmacy, her Aunt Ruth had enjoyed checking out the flowers in the yard. The azaleas under the massive oak tree were starting to bloom, tulips and other spring flowers were poking their heads out of the ground. Early that morning, she watched birds as they called to each other from the branches. Later in the day as she sat in the white rocker on her front porch drinking her coffee she watched them as they carried twigs to build nests.

"This is my favorite time of year. I always loved the time when winter is over and the weather was warm enough to open the windows and let the breezes chase the stale air out and fill the house with fresh air," Ruth smiled. Lydia blew her a kiss when she left for work.

"Aunt Ruth looks especially happy this morning."

At the evening meal the night before Ruth had talked about how full her life had been because of Lydia. Even though she had never married she called Lydia her daughter. Ruth, who was really Lydia's mother's aunt, was a spry seventy two years old when she took Lydia in and raised her as her own. "Right then and there is when I knew it was time for me to retire from teaching. God had given me a more important job." She said.

It was 6:30 in the morning. Ruth was usually already up and making coffee by this time. So when Lydia went in to check on her, she had an uneasy feeling of what she would find. When she peeked in Ruth looked peaceful as if she were still sleeping. She had been telling Lydia that she couldn't live forever.

"When my time comes, honey, I don't want you to mourn. I have lived a long and full life. I enjoyed the years God allowed me to stay on this earth. Ok, you can shed **one** tear. Then laugh as you remember all the good times we have had together. Remember the trips we took. Remember especially the trip to Italy, to Rome, the Sistine Chapel. Remember that day we wandered around on the back streets of Venice and had to back track because there was no other way out. Remember the quiet times we have had here at home, the times we just sat in silence enjoying each other."

As one lone tear slid down her face, Lydia did laugh as memories flooded her mind. "Aunt Ruth, you wise old owl, I really do love you."

The first person she called was Kate Jackson Gray, her best friend in high school who now lived in Minnesota. Kate, Lydia's long time friend had flown in as soon as she got the call. Samuel told Kate to go ahead and he would take care of the cancelations for both of them. He promised to come later in time for the funeral. Kate met Samuel Gray, a medical doctor, when she went there to study psychology at the university. Their wedding took place in Windfield before she moved to his home state and set up separate practices. Aunt Ruth called them the alphabet girls because they called each other Kay and Dee. Even though they now lived far apart, they kept in contact and still considered themselves best friends.

"There were so many people at Aunt Ruth's funeral the whole town must have come," Kate Gray commented, "She taught most of them. I remember her saying that the children of the whole town were her children."

The funeral was held at 11:00 that morning. As was the custom in Winfield, the mourners gathered back at the house where the dining table had been filled with food by friends. The table was covered with casserole dishes, cakes, pies, roast beef, fried chicken, and breads of all kinds. Friends, neighbors and the women of Ruth's church had brought the usual fare to show their respect to the family.

Later, several friends and neighbors including Kate, Samuel and Leroy were still there sitting in their favorite room, the neat and clean cozy kitchen, drinking coffee, and sharing stories about 'Aunt Ruth' 'as she was called by most who knew her.

The house had been built by Ruth's parents in the early 1900's. Ruth and Lydia took good care of it and kept up with repairs and maintenance. Therefore it was in very good shape. And it still held several pieces of her parent's furniture. They still used her 'electric range' and metal table and padded chair set that Ruth bought for the kitchen when Lydia came to live with her. "This will be a special place for us to share milk and cookies, our thoughts and feelings and plan activities. I have always felt more at home in the kitchen than in the formal dining room which has a cold and stilted feeling."

Two straight back chairs were against the wall between the two windows. Light from these windows made the kitchen bright and cheery. Ruth didn't like dark rooms, "Sunlight chases away the gloomies." Looking out the windows you could see the garden which grew fresh vegetables. The stand-alone sink had been converted into a cabinet with Formica counter tops and hanging cabinets. Her mother's old white pie safe which now held dishes stood in the corner. Because the porcelain top was cool it was the best place to make breads and pie crusts. Lydia had painted blue-violet irises with light green leaves on leaning stems on the doors. An old but still serviceable refrigerator was on the right of the safe. A small counter topped storage closet was near the range on the inside wall of the kitchen. Just beyond the range was the back door which led to a small porch.

"There's plenty of cake and pie if anyone would like it to go with your coffee," Lydia offered. "I don't think the refrigerator will hold it all. We do have good cooks and it would be a shame to let it go to waste. If I try to eat any more it will go to waist. So you are expected to help me out by carrying some with you."

After the funeral and all the friends had gone, Lydia sat in the Queen Anne chair in her small bedroom with Kate. Sam, knowing that the two friends would like to be alone had checked in the local hotel. He had declined the invitation to stay with Leroy at his parent's farm. He confided to Lydia, "I think it best to stay at the hotel because Leroy seems uncomfortable around us. I sense that he is jealous of your friendship with Kate."

DANGEROUS OCCUPATION

Before Kate and Samuel left to return home she advised Lydia to wait a year before making any important decisions.

A week after all her guests had gone Lydia was sitting on the front porch missing everyone when Leroy drove up. "I thought you could use a little company. From the sad look on your face I think I'm right." He walked up and took her in his arms. Lydia leaned down and put her head on his shoulder, "Oh Leroy, I miss her so much. I just don't know what to do. I know she was getting old. I know she lived a long and full life. We even talked about this but I just didn't know how much it would hurt."

"Now don't you worry your pretty head about anything. I am here and I will take care of you," consoled Leroy. "I will help you get your Aunt Ruth's will probated. I had to go through that when my parents died. Do you know where the will is? It should be filed with her lawyer. Do you know what is in it? I'm sure she left her property to you. I'll help you take care of the finances. I know women aren't good at these things."

When Lydia pulled back and frowned at him, he went on to say, "Oh, but you are good at other things. Just let me go over the books. I'll see to it that you aren't cheated by some fast talking lawyer."

"That's sweet of you but I think I can handle it. Yes, Aunt Ruth had a will. We discussed it and she gave me instructions as to its contents and how she wanted everything handled so there shouldn't be any problem. It's a simple will and probate shouldn't take much time."

Then his words began to hit home. It shocked her. She had been touched by his visit to comfort her. Then he had to go and spoil it. "Aunt Ruth took care of things herself. I hope you didn't mean to sound so self-righteous. Women aren't as simpleminded as you might think. I can read and I don't need you to take care of me!"

"Hey, don't get so upset sweetheart. I just want to help. You were so sad and alone when I came I just felt you may not be thinking as clearly as you usually do. Really I just want to help. We all could use help every once in a while especially at a time such as this. I know how close you and your Aunt Ruth were. I want you to know I am here for you just like you would be here for me if I needed you."

"I'm sorry I over reacted Leroy. You are right we do need each other." She reached over and kissed him on the cheek.

They sat on the porch swing for awhile swinging in silence. "I hate to break up this rousing conversation." Leroy laughed as he rose, but there are a few chores at home that need my attention."

Lydia laughed too as she rose to walk him to his truck but he stayed on the porch with his hands in his back pockets. "Lydia, come home with me. I hate to leave you here all alone. You know I can't stay here. I need to go home but you could come with me. After I take care of the animals we could spend some time together and you wouldn't be here alone with your grief."

Lydia did feel lonely and was tempted, "Thanks but No Leroy, I should get back to my work. There are several jobs that I have promised to do. It's time for me to get myself together and join the living. That's what I promised Aunt Ruth."

A little over a year after Ruth passed away, Lydia and Leroy married. This was no surprise because most everyone in Winfield expected them to wed someday.

Chapter 7

AFTER AUNT RUTH DIED LYDIA was advised by her friends not to make important decisions until a year had passed. She was lost because all her life had been centered around her Aunt Ruth. The year passed quickly as Lydia took care of the normal business of probate and transferring property into her name. The will was simple. Ruth left the money in her savings account to *The House of Shiphrah,* a children's home she helped to set up. The rest, her house and 5 acres of land, was left to Lydia.

The will was no surprise to Lydia. Her Aunt Ruth had already given her instruction as to the distribution of her worldly goods. Ruth had always felt that Lydia could take care of herself. But there were little ones that had no family or the family was unable to care for a child. These children needed a safe and secure place to live. As a little child Lydia was told the stories of the Bible. Even her name, Lydia, was taken from the Bible. After hearing about babies dying because of neglect or abuse, Ruth decided to set up the *Shiphrah House* where young mothers who could not care for their babies could come and get the help needed.

A year later Lydia was getting settled in her new routine. She filled her days with work. There were many businesses that wanted her to set up inventive displays. She had been asked by Windfield Contractor and Remodeling Company to work for them on a permanent basis. She had used she skills as an interior designer in several of their new homes. But taking her friend Kay's advice she was waiting for a year after the loss of Aunt Ruth before making any big decisions. She also liked the idea of working with different companies and making her own decisions by working free lance. She worked long hours and was so tired that she hardly had time to dwell on the past. When she fell into bed at night she thanked God for the talents He had given her and the ability to do what she loved. She fell asleep thinking of all the good times she and her Aunt Ruth had shared.

Lydia was setting up a new display in the pharmacy window when Mr. Partain called from the back. "Lydia, I need you." When she entered the storage room, she found Bob leaning against the desk.

"Goodness you are white as a sheet. What's wrong?"

'I just don't feel up to par right now. Susan stepped out to mail some letters. Do you think you can handle things here for awhile? I think I'll just go home and rest a minute."

"Oh no you won't", Lydia sat down and looked him in the eye. "You are going to go straight to the doctor. I am going to put a sign on the door that I will be back shortly. I will leave you with the Doctor and return to the pharmacy. Susan should be back by then. It's almost closing time anyway."

As soon as she returned to the pharmacy, Susan, the ever protective secretary, rushed to her, "What's going on? Where is Bob? This isn't like you to close and leave the pharmacy. What if a customer had come? Where's Bob?" Her voice got higher at each question.

Lydia explained what happened and after closing they both went back to check on Bob. The doctor had finished and was explaining that he needed to slow down.

"I just hate it when doctors say 'You're getting on in years you know.'Just give him a few more years. Some doctor will be telling him that. You are just as old as you feel. Course I don't feel that young at the moment." He laughed.

A few months later Bob asked Susan and Lydia to sit down. He explained that he had been thinking of retiring for awhile and the trip to the doctor just clinched it. "Heck I may just take up fishing. I might even find that I like it. I guess 75 isn't too old to try something new. Now Susan here has been staying on to help me out. She's no spring chicken herself.' He ducked as Susan swatted at him.

"So what do you say let's put a "Gone fishing" sign on the door and close up shop." They laughed and spent the rest of the day teasing about retiring to go fishing, swinging on the porch swing, sitting in a rocker wrapped in an old quilt, and sipping soup through a straw.

As Lydia walked home that evening she thought of Aunt Ruth and how things were changing. She missed talking in the evening about her work and things that happened during the day. She was going to miss working at the pharmacy. It was like her family. This would mean that she would be short one paycheck. But she did have her other jobs that kept her busy. After seeing the displays in the window of the pharmacy, she had been asked by other businesses to help them out from time to time. She knew how to manage her finances God was still with her and all would work out. She gave herself a pep talk, placed a smile on her face and with a lighter spirit walked briskly the rest of the way home.

After she arrived at home her mood changed.

Lydia felt a stab to her heart as she looked around the place that had been her whole life. All seemed to be gone in a flash her Aunt Ruth was gone, her job at the pharmacy had been terminated, Old Ben was getting too frail to keep up with the never ending job of maintenance.

Even though the house had been built by Aunt Ruth's Father, it had been kept in good repair by a good friend who was handy with tools. "Uncle Ben" had been a friend as long as Lydia could remember. He always seemed to be there when there was "man's work" to be done. The yard was large and sported six large oak trees. An assortment of flowers grew around each tree. There were low growing flowering shrubs around the house. In back was the garden that produced fresh vegetables for the table and enough to can for winter. The green lawn that Ben had planted and kept trimmed finished the description of the cozy cottage.

Later that month Lydia and Leroy had gone as usual to a Saturday afternoon movie. As they walked to her house Lydia looked up and laughed, "Looks like rain. Race you. Last one to the house cooks supper."

"Hurry up slow poke." She smiled as she hugged the front porch post. "I won and you cook."

"I don't think so. Do you want us both to get sick?" huffed Leroy as he wrestled them both to the ground. They rushed into the house just as the downpour started.

"Would you look at that dark cloud?" Lydia exclaimed to Leroy, as she prepared an early supper for them. "I'd better hurry in case the electricity goes out. Hey, a candlelight supper might be nice. But on the other hand raw steak wouldn't. Oh well, can't have everything, can we?"

"Candle light? Hey I like to see what I am eating," Laughed Leroy.

"Well it was just a thought. You know I don't like the look of that sky. It is getting darker. Do you think a storm is brewing?" It was easy for Lydia to see the clouds out the kitchen windows.

"You're right it is getting darker. Looks like it will be rough going getting home tonight. Maybe I need to leave right after supper. Anyway, I like to get home early because I have to get up early to tend to the animals."

"In that case, I guess I need to hurry with supper. I gathered fresh vegetables this morning and planned to have green beans for supper because I know you like them. But I think I'll steam these fresh vegetables instead of the green beans since that will be faster. I won't cook cornbread as planned. Maybe we should eat now. If you get down the dishes and I will put the food on the table"

Leroy was reaching for the dishes in the cabinet when there was flash of lightning and a big clap of thunder immediately followed. He turned, grabbed Lydia and ran with her to the hall just as a large oak tree crashed into the kitchen.

"Lydia, are you okay? Did I hurt you? It was so sudden I didn't have time to think. I just grabbed you and ran." They were holding onto each other in shock.

They sat there huddled in the dark. The storm had moved on but there were flashes of lightning in the distance. "I have emergency candles but they are in the kitchen.' The rain had slowed but there was water still coming in where a limb struck through the roof.

"We do need light to see how bad things are. Okay I'll go in there and get the candles," offered Leroy. "Where are they?"

"No it would be easier for me to go in and get them than tell you where they are."

DANGEROUS OCCUPATION

I'll go with you. It may be dangerous. It'd dark and that limb may not be stable"

"Don't be silly. There is no need for both of us getting drenched. Besides I know exactly where there are. I can see when the lightning flashes. I'll just move when I can see where I'm going. I'll be right back."

She returned with a plastic box which contained candles, candle holder, and matches. They worked their way into the living area where it was fairly dry, put the candle on a table and bent over to light candle. They stood close together and cupped hands around it to keep out the draft.

"Leroy?"

"What?"

"Why are we whispering?" They laughed so hard he could hardly light the candle.

As they went from room to room they could see water dripping from every room except the Lydia's bedroom and her bathroom. Lydia talked Leroy into gathering a few pictures from Aunt Ruth's old bedroom and put them into a trunk. Each took hold of a strap on the end and carried it to Lydia's room.

"Now what do I do?" she sighed as she sank down on the trunk.

"Hello," came a voice from the front. Is anyone hurt in here? We're from the fire department checking out the neighborhood to see if anyone needs help." A beam of light was in front of the voice. The light landed on a very wet but grateful couple.

She could almost hear a sigh of relief from Leroy when Lydia politely refused his offer to stay at his house. She didn't know the condition of the house but with him living alone she assumed that it wasn't good.

Lydia's insurance paid for her stay in a hotel while the damages were assessed. The house had suffered such structural damage that it wasn't feasible to repair or remodel.

So Leroy's solution was to get married. "We can use the insurance to build a starter house which shouldn't take too long especially since you have connections with that building contractor you know. Later we can build our 'dream house'."

The house was built on Leroy's farm. The contractor, Todd Merck, was the friend who had hired Lydia to do interior decorating in some of his buildings. Lydia thought it would be wonderful to live in the country where she could enjoy the animals and wild flowers there. The house was small and the furnishing meager since there was little time to plan. And besides 'they were going to build a dream house later'.

The wedding took place shortly after the house was finished and the necessary furnishings were in place. It was held in Windfield First Church and the reception was held in the civic center. Because of the short time to plan the wedding there was an open invitation to everyone to attend. Most of the people in town expected to be invited anyway because Lydia was well known and loved. Her friends made the wedding event a community project. Lydia paid for the materials and they supplied the labor. Matty catered the event and Mark, Matty's husband was the photographer. Alice did her hair and makeup. The local seamstress out-did herself when she made the elegant flowing white gown decorated with white beads with princess style scoop neckline. Lydia wore her pearl beads and earrings that had been saved from the storm because they were in her bedroom. The local florist made the arrangements. The town's local band supplied the music. The jeweler gave Lydia a substantial discount on the wedding rings. Bob Partain, Lydia's former boss who was like a father to her gave her away. Kate who was the bride's maid flew down from Minnesota with Samuel. As the bridal party was getting dressed Kate announced that she was pregnant. It was a beautiful celebration that lasted far into the night. Leroy said the honeymoon would have to wait because he couldn't leave the farm at that time.

So Lydia set up housekeeping on the farm and started drawing plans for her future house. It would be a white two story structure. The house would be built near the large oak trees that were already on the farm. This was a perfect spot with the oak trees and in back a small stream that bubbled over large slabs of slate. She would landscape it with azaleas and camellias. There would be summer flower beds in front of the white two story antebellum house. The foyer would be wide with light coming from windows on each side of the large front door. Just beyond the entry way would be winding stairs, white with cherry rails. A chandelier would hang from the high ceiling. The kitchen would be state of the art. The appliances would be stainless steel. There would be an open brick fireplace at waist level with a spit for roasting large roasts. This would be great for cooking meals for the friends she planned to entertain. The dining area would be just off the kitchen. This would not be a formal dining room but one where everyone could feel at home and enjoy the meals she planned to serve. There would be light coming in from side windows that looked out over the back where the oaks and stream was. She also started planning how she would decorate the new house. She was so happy and looked forward to a long and happy life on this beautiful land with Leroy.

Chapter 8

"You sure did look funny loping over them clods as you ran across my plowed field with your dress just a 'flapping in the wind", laughed Leroy as he sat down to take off his work boots then switched to his recliner to sit and reread the paper. It amused Lydia that he sat in his favorite chair, and then moved over to the recliner. This was part his routine as he sat in the "shrine to his parents".

The rocker was in the part of the room that Lydia called "Leroy's corner". It was an aging plastic covered slide rocker with small faded pink flowers.

"This is the rocker that my mother used to rock me to sleep when I was a baby". He always reminded her when she complained that it was an eyesore. Lydia tired of trying to keep the chair clean. It had ridges to make it look like cloth but it just caught the grime that Leroy was forever bringing in from the field.

"*Why does he get such a delight in making fun of me at every turn?*" thought Lydia as she placed the last biscuit in the pan and put it in the hot oven to bake. She then cleaned the counter, washed and dried her hands and stirred the green beans that she had just picked fresh from the garden. "*Here I am working hard to fix a good meal for him and all he does is make fun of me as I hurry to bring him cool water to drink. It is his crazy idea that women should not wear pants. The gospel according to the good Reverend Goodman is that men should wear the pants in the family."*

Lydia had been out in the garden gathering vegetables for dinner when she rushed in the house to answer the phone. It was Leroy calling from his cell phone to tell her to bring him some cold water.

"There is no need to tell Leroy that I am too busy to stop what I am doing to carry water to him. It would just start his cussing again about women's place in the family and man being head of the household as written in the Bible. He could carry water with him but, oh no that would be too much, besides that it would not be cold.

Lydia looked around the kitchen with the meager furnishings. It was as if he had totally forgotten about the house he promised when they married. Because her house had been damaged in a storm, this house was to be temporary housing until her dream house was built. She had long since put aside her new house plans that she had worked on just after they were married. Leroy had insisted on providing just the necessary appliances with which to prepare meals. The floor was of rustic planks "because it lasted longer and was good enough for my parents." Leroy made fun of "fancy throw rugs or frilly curtains spread out all over the place". Lydia had gone along with the simple furnishings because she thought it was until the new house was built. She had let it slide for five years now and Leroy seemed to be settled in this house.

Lydia liked to make the house pretty but Leroy always found some fault with her efforts. He had told her that she was putting on airs and trying to "think herself better than she ought, which is written in the Bible also". There had been little change since the house was built when they married. The Formica counter top was white with gold and silver specks. The golden yellow oven and refrigerator were so old the color had turned to a ugly dark goldenrod. The table, which sat just beyond the kitchen counter, was a plain pine with oak finish. Six oak chairs sat around the table. On the table was a simple pale yellow tablecloth. She would not go along with the felt backed oil cloth that Leroy liked. "She picked her fights carefully and this was one she would win", she had told her friend, Sophie. The den was just beyond the kitchen. A couch faced "Leroy's Corner" where Leroy liked to sit which was on the right side of the kitchen. This area was open with no walls between.

The den was furnished with a brown and orange couch with wooden arms" a fight lost", two end tables and two matching lamps and a rough plank coffee table. Lydia did not like the typical matching end tables with matching lamps that everyone seemed to have. She wanted to decorate the house to fit her own personality, but was willing to give in because she also liked a peaceful house. She made throw pillows of a soft gold color to cover some of the ugly brown couch.

A large screen TV sat in the corner facing the gosh-awful chair. Behind the chair was "another fight lost" sat an anvil that had been Leroy's grandfather's. The chair and anvil sat in the middle of the den and had been the source of many arguments that Lydia lost. The anvil was too heavy to move when she tried to clean the floor. Even when she got mad enough to move it herself, it was just too heavy to move. Leroy had insisted that it stay in the house. Lydia wanted to put it in the barn "where it belonged". "The anvil and chair are part of my heritage and they stay!"

As Lydia sat the table with light green placemats and matching napkins, she wondered what had happened to their marriage. It seemed that they had different ideas of what a marriage is. She envisioned a life together as partners. His idea was the man being the head of the household and the wife as a helper. (Genesis 2:20 KJV ---"but for Adam there was not found a help meet for him.") He failed to notice that there is a note in the Study Bible saying that 'meet' means 'fit'. After reading and rereading this creation story, Lydia noticed that every animal had a match except Adam. So God made a match for him.

When Lydia pointed this out to Leroy he accused her of twisting the scriptures to fit her own ideas.

"This is getting me nowhere.' Lydia shook her head. Thinking about all this just gets me down." She went over to pick up the cotton weight that was always falling off the wall. "No! I'll just leave it there. There is no reason why I should have to pick it up anyway. My goodness what is wrong with me? Why do I resent little things like this? Is Leroy right? Is it my fault that things have gone so wrong? *Please God, give me an answer,*" she prayed.

After that Lydia tried to get advice without going to anyone she knew. When the subject of marriage and how to make relationships work came up in Sunday School she made sure to ask generic questions, questions that would provide feedback and information about God's word without calling attention to her personal situation. The general consensus seemed to be that if you were meek, mild and accommodating you would receive it back. If you lashed out in anger that is what you would get back. So Lydia decided to do more study on the subject on line. She looked up works by some of the ministers listed in the Sunday School books they used in church. She gleaned information from any source she could get.

Lydia was listening to a sermon on TV as she cleaned the house. The subject was the difference between men and women and how they view things differently especially when it came to discussions or disagreements. Men seem to take offence when a woman says "We need to talk". Men see this as an affront to his manhood and the wife wants to find fault. The woman sees this as a chance to clear the air and explain how she feels about something. The advice was to find a time when both are calm before bringing up a controversial topic. When either is angry is no time to try to solve a problem.

Another problem is that wives seem to think men are mind readers and should know what is troubling her. The advice was to tell the husband what you want and don't expect the husband to understand why you are angry at him.

That evening after supper dishes had been put away she decided to talk with Leroy who was sitting quietly in his recliner. It seemed to be the right time to bring up a subject that had been weighing heavily on her mind for quite a while. She was aggravated but promised herself to approach the topic calmly and in a nonthreatening manner. She dried her hands on the hand towel and went over to sit near him in her wingback chair.

"Leroy it has been five years since we married and you have worked hard all this time without a break. I was wondering if it is now time to take that honeymoon that we never got around to when we married. I thought that after you finish gathering the winter feed we could take a trip somewhere. I have mapped out a sightseeing trip which would take us about a week. I know you haven't seen much of our country and it would be fun."

In the last few years Leroy had become settled in his ways and saw no need to be affectionate. Lydia thought that getting away from the work on the farm might put a spark back in their relationship. When she had tried to show affection Leroy had shunned the effort saying he was tired since he had been working all day. She was hurt when he was so cold toward her. Each time she tried and was rejected it made the hurt go deeper. When she tried to put a little spice in the marriage by dressing in a skimpy nighty, Leroy did not even notice it.

So this was the reason she tried to plan a trip. She would use the advice she had gleaned from all the sources and give it another try. She had heard that the only person that you can change is yourself. This made a lot of sense so she tried another tactic. She thought if she made it easy by doing all the planning Leroy would agree to a short trip. She talked with Sammy, who ran the feed store and had a farm as well, and arranged for him to look after things if they took a vacation.

"I have asked Sammy if he would look after things here. So you wouldn't have to worry about that. Wouldn't it be fun to see some of the good old USA?"

"You did what? Yelled Leroy as he half rose out of his easy chair. "You mean you went behind my back and took matters in your own hand? I'm head of this household. What must Sammy think of me? He must think I'm some sort of hen pecked weakling not capable of running my own business. Do you know how this makes me look?"

Then he settled back down in his chair and took out a magazine to read. "Anyway I have already promised to look after the McCoy farm while they visit with his wife's family. So I can't possibly get away. Next time you want to make plans for me let me know." He sat back and began thumbing through the magazine.

Lydia was devastated. She now saw her future as one of loneliness and drudgery. She could see her life being whiled away with nothing to look forward to but working in the house and garden and running errands for Leroy.

She walked into the spare bedroom and slumped down on the bed. She had tried to bring life back into the marriage to no avail. She was so heartbroken she stayed in the spare bedroom that night. She had fallen asleep sometime way into the night.

The next morning Leroy went about his usual routine as if nothing had happened. In his mind things had been settled. They were not going anywhere. Lydia just couldn't shake her depressed feelings. She had prayed for help but it seemed that God wasn't listening. She had done everything in her power to make things better. She was trying to be a good wife. She was trying to be a good Christian. She had looked for help and understanding by doing research. After Leroy left the house she began to cry. The more she tried to stop the worse thing got. She began to sob uncontrollably. She went into the spare bedroom and crumpled into a corner. She was heartbroken. Her life seemed to be over. There was nothing to look forward to. Ahead of her was day after day of nothingness.

Leroy saw that she had been crying that afternoon but didn't say anything. But he did make an attempt at being nice by thanking her for a good meal.

After that she spent most of her evenings in the spare bedroom reading or working on designs on her computer. The computer was supplied by the construction company when she did work on their projects. She knew that it was up to her to find a way to compensate and fill her life. She knew it was up to her to change. She would have to accept things as they were because there was no changing Leroy. She would have to decide what she was willing to put up with and what was worth an argument. If she was going to stay in the marriage she would have to change or accept. If she continued to hope Leroy would change she would be fooling herself. Being a dutiful wife was not working. The more she let Leroy have his way the more he expected it. It was partly her fault because she had not stood up to him before now. Letting him make decisions for them both had just made him more controlling. He was now treating her as if she had no brain at all. It was so bad that he was now telling her how to wash dishes. She had allowed him to take over because she did not like strife and Leroy had a short fuse. He could lose his temper over the least little thing, especially if it came to his pride in being the man of the house. It was at the point now where they hardly ever had a conversation. He read the paper, a magazine or watched television. When Lydia tried to make conversation by asking how his day went or about what he was reading, he gave a short answer like 'working' or 'nothing much'. It was as if what he did was a secret. Was this the way it would be the rest of her life?

Chapter 9

It was late September Leroy had sent her into town to get a part for the tractor. While driving into Windfield, Lydia couldn't help but enjoy the beauty of God's handiwork. Along the highway trees displayed a medley of color. The hickory nut trees radiated a golden brown. Maples shaped like hot air balloons sported a green interior with red outer layer. Closer into town the burnt orange crape myrtles were stretching upward. As she passed the houses she was reminded of her childhood home. The fall flowering shrubs in an array of pinks and reds were bordered by white, yellow, and orange mums. She felt so at peace and close to God she whispered a thank you prayer for the beauty all around her.

This made Lydia daydream of decorating her house. She liked to change things around to make it different. But Leroy did not like for her to change the furniture. He liked his corner just the way it was. She could feel a cloud of despair descend to cover her sunny mood.

"Okay Lydia enough of that," she told herself. "Here you were enjoying God's handiwork and you go and ruin it with your gray thoughts."

"I know just what to do to cheer me up," she told herself out loud. "Why don't I stop by the feed store while I'm in town and see Sammy and Missy?" Melissa started helping Sammy with the store after he bought it.

Lydia felt much better after visiting with the Evans family. Sammy had called Melissa who brought over the twin girls, May and June. They had wanted to name a child after Lydia but after the twins were born in two different months they felt it only natural to name them after the month they were born. May was born at 11:57, May 31st and June was born at 12:05, June 1st. The news media had a field day with that. It was even in national news.

"That was such a nice visit. I know I stayed too long but it was great." Right then and there she vowed to stop with her sad thoughts. "I know that I am the only person that I can change. So if I want to be happy I have to decide what I am willing to put up with, change what I can and put up with what I can't. The rest of the week she tried not to let Leroy's comments get to her.

After attending Beulah Land Church that Sunday she made a stab at pleasant conversation. Leroy was sitting in his corner reading the Sunday edition of the news while she prepared the noonday meal. He looked up "Boy, that was some sermon this morning. He really was on fire. He sure let those sinners have it."

Lydia didn't answer because she didn't like the sermon. Preaching against sin is what preachers should do but his lambasting in a monotone voice just grated on her nerves. *"I know I shouldn't be so judgmental. I am doing what I dislike about Rev. Goodman's sermons,"* she thought. "I don't know what it is that get's to me but I come home from church feeling worse that when I went. I never felt that way when I went to Windfield First in Town. I always felt refreshed and ready to serve the Lord. *"Okay it is up to me to change the subject."*

"Wasn't that a snappy suit that Mr. Grant was wearing today? I wonder where he shops. You sure would look good in one like it."

"What?" stormed Leroy. 'What are you doing looking at another man?" Leroy was glaring at her. She was so shocked that she stopped what she was doing in the kitchen.

"But I just thought how nice you would look in one like it." "So much for pleasant conversation." she said under her breath.

It was no surprise that the sermon the next Sunday was on lust of the flesh. *"Those Tuesday morning breakfasts with Leroy sure gives the good reverend a lot of preaching material,"* thought Lydia as she sat in the pew. *"This sermon isn't making me feel like I am in worship. I need to turn my thoughts around and try to get a message out of it."*

That's when the sermon turned to the short dresses that women and girls wear and how it makes men lust after them. "Men can't help but look if women show themselves," boomed the preacher. That's when Lydia tuned him out and started planning the next design that she was working on for a fall display.

"Lester, did you notice the preacher glaring at us when he was talking about lusting after another man's wife?" asked Betty. The Grants were walking toward their car after as they left the church. "I wonder what that was all about."

"Well no, I didn't notice that but I did notice that people were not as friendly toward us as they usually are." He took his wife's hand and kissed it, "Don't let it bother you sweetheart. Maybe it's just our imagination." He let out a hearty laugh, "The preacher sure put a bee in the hats of some. Can't you hear the speculation going on around the dinner tables today at home and the telephones ringing off the hooks? That bee hive will really be humming. You know how some people in the church like to gossip." They were still laughing when they arrived at home.

The next Sunday morning during announcements, Rev Goodman asked for a show of hands of those willing to go visiting, witnessing on Tuesday. *"Leroy must have had prior knowledge of this announcement because his hand was up before the words were out o his mouth,"* Lydia thought as she squirmed in her seat. This was not something she was comfortable in doing. She never felt God wanted her knock on people's door to tell them what a sinner they were. When God gave her an opening she shared her love of God and what He has done for her in her life.

On Tuesday, the group met Leroy at his house. They all trooped in, Bibles under the arm, and smiles plastered on each face ready to attack any sinner they met.

"Why don't you come with us?" Bessie and Essie chimed together. Lydia shook her head "No, I think I will skip this activity" Lydia answered with a polite smile.

"God laid it on my heart to say this. I think you need to search your heart to find out why you will not spread the word," Amy spoke up.

"Oh yes", came from Henryetta, "We can't help but worry about your soul."

"Well, I just talked with God a few minutes ago and He didn't say a word about speaking to you about me." *I can't believe I said that.* Lydia failed to mention that what she had said a few minutes ago was, "Oh my lord here they **all** come."

"Well, I never!" the good reverend broke in, "I think it's time we left this house." As he left he made a point to wipe his feet on the welcome mat as he said something about shaking the dust off his feet. *"From the looks of my clean floor, I wish they all had wiped their feet before they **came** in." I guess I shouldn't have said that but they can be such know it alls. Oh well, the good reverend will have a month's worth of sermons on my behavior alone.*

Chapter 10

LYDIA WORKED BEHIND THE SCREENS in Sims' Department Store display window. Every Christmas she worked in secret to create a Christmas scene. As people walked by they couldn't help but speculate on what she was come up with this year. The unveiling was to be Saturday two weeks before Christmas. This seemed to set the mood for shopping for that special gift. "Lydia's Creation is coming soon" was printed on the partition that was set up to hide her work.

The daily news carried a feature story about Lydia and her annual Christmas gift to the town.

"This year it is going to be better than ever." thought Lydia. She was so excited because she felt it was going to be the town's best Christmas present she had ever created.

Over the years after she had set up displays in Partain's Pharmacy and Alice's beauty shop she had been asked to create displays in several other businesses.

Sims' Department Store had 2 display windows. One Lydia tried to keep current with different scenes, but the other was used for sales throughout the year except for the Christmas special display.

The left window was used to display a family in different activities in keeping with the seasons or holiday at the time. This month the family was shown going on an outing to the woods to get a Christmas tree.

DANGEROUS OCCUPATION

There are two conveyor belts working in sequence. The window was set up with evergreen trees with snow on the ground. The family emerged on the right. They were dressed for cold winter weather. The father has an ax resting on his shoulder. A boy and girl with excited expressions race before the father and the mother is following. The family crosses to the midpoint of the window and disappears toward the back. Then a sound of an ax cutting down a tree can be heard. After that the family appears out of the middle dragging a tree. The family then disappears on the left. Lydia has placed the trees so that the two tracks are hidden from view. This gave the town something to look at while she worked on her special Christmas window.

Finally the awaited day arrives for the showing of the window on the right, Lydia's Christmas gift. Children of the community had been given a chance to sign up for the drawing to see who would be the one to pull the curtain on the display. Lydia, of course was there to make sure all went as planned.

The curtain was pulled showing a Christmas scene: Each section had moving pieces powered by batteries in conjunction with a computer. In a corner of the living room is a Christmas tree being decorated by the father and two children. Cars race on a track around the tree. Mother is sipping from a cup. In the background on a table is a manger scene. A little girl sits on the floor with a box and as she turns the handle a clown pops up. The little girl topples over with laughter. Grandmother is rocking in a rocking chair; nearby a cat is lapping milk from a bowl. Each time Grandmother rocks the cat's swishing tail gets caught and squeezes air into the cat which in turn makes the cat's hair stand on end. Each time the rocker lets up the cat returns to normal and laps at the milk.

This last activity caused some to question whether Lydia should have the cat getting caught by the rocker. Some thought it was funny and the cat wasn't really hurt because he goes back to drinking milk. Someone in the crowd said that this was a cruel act and children should not be exposed to it. Lydia didn't see who has made that comment.

Lydia explained that most everyone has seen the rocking chair with the cat's tail moving just in time to be missed. She thought that she would do something different. Most of the people in the crowd agreed that it was indeed funny. Several came by to tell her that they loved the display and thanked her for her annual Christmas gift to the town. That's why she was so surprised to see a write-up in the newspaper the next morning. Rev. Bradley Goodman was quoted as saying that the entire crowd was aghast at the sadistic display that Lydia had set up for the whole town to see.

Chapter 11

Things were getting better at home because Lydia ignored some of the things that had previously upset her. She cooked meals that she knew Leroy liked and made pleasant conversation. She cleaned and dusted around Leroy's corner as much as possible and tried to leave it like he wanted it. She decorated in areas where she thought he would not mind.

Lydia was determined to change. She had decided to try to understand the lessons being explained in the Sunday morning sermons. She would enter the church with a better attitude. She would try to be an asset not a hindrance.

She saw her chance to make a difference when the church had a business meeting. For some time there had been a problem with the stage that moved electronically. The company that sold them the stage had long since gone out of business and no one seemed to be able to replace parts that were needed. One of the members of the building and grounds committee had found a gear that was just a little larger than the original part. A motion was made to use this part. During the discussion that followed it was explained that other gears would be shifted over a little to make it fit.

Lydia stood up, "Mr. Moderator?"

"Uh, Uh, Mrs. Martin," stuttered the moderator.

"If you use the larger gear the stage may be ripped apart," Explained Lydia.

"MISSES MARTIN PLEASE SIT DOWN," yelled Rev. Goodman.

Lydia gasped and looked around. All eyes were huge orbs looking at her. "What? What's wrong?"

"MR. MARTIN PLEASE ESCORT YOUR WIFE OUTSIDE."

Leroy rose from his seat. His face was beet red. He took Lydia by the arm and with force led her out of the church. "Why do you insist on embarrassing me in front of the entire church?"

"What in heaven's name did I do?" Lydia had stopped in her tracks even though Leroy was tugging her toward the car.

"You need to read your Bible", Leroy was grinding his teeth. He put her in the car and slammed the door. They went the rest of the way home in silence. When he got home he reached for the Bible. Lydia was afraid to upset him more and decided to wait to find out what she did that was so wrong. So she set the table and waited for the roast to finish cooking. She had put it on to cook while they were in church. But since they came home early it was not quite done. She noticed that Leroy was flipping pages in the Bible so she went out to sit on the porch.

When she went back in Leroy had put the Bible down. "Now that you have calmed down, I want to know what that was all about." She asked quietly.

"The Bible says that women should not to speak out in church. Being the 'educated woman' you think you are I would think you knew that. Now I'll be the talk of the town. It'll probably be spread all over tomorrow's paper. You'll have to apologize to the preacher and ask forgiveness from the church."

"Oh, are you talking about 1 Timothy 2:11 where Paul gave instructions to Timothy about the women of Ephesus?" she turned around toward the kitchen so Leroy could not see her face. She grinned as she thought, *"So that's what he was looking for."* She picked up the roast and put it on the table.

She continued as she sat down, "That passage appears to be Paul warning Timothy about sound teaching in Ephesus. There seemed to be some in that church, including pushy women, who were involved in unsound teaching. There are other places in the Bible where women helped in spreading the teachings of Jesus. Leroy I'm not trying to preach to you. I am just trying to let you know what I read when I read that passage. But when it comes to my speaking out in the meeting, I just thought I would be of help in the matter of the stage since I do have a knowledge of mechanics."

After the meal and dishes were done she went out on the porch where Leroy was sitting. "Leroy, I just don't seem to fit in at Beulah Land Church. Now I am beginning to understand a lot of things about the church services. I wondered why women haven't been called on to pray. I'm truly sorry if I embarrassed you. I would never do that. The church I grew up in was more open to women. Everyone who professed Christ as Lord was treated as Christian brothers and sisters. I'm not saying we were perfect but no one was treated like he or she was less than any other. Since I am not to speak in church I will write an apology that you can read. I will say that I am sorry for the misunderstanding and for any hard feelings that my words caused."

The next Sunday Lydia got ready early and handed Leroy the apology. "I will not be going with you. I will be going to Windfield First." She walked out before Leroy had time to respond.

For years Leroy and Rev. Goodman had been meeting on Tuesday morning at Matty's Diner for breakfast. Sometimes other men from the church would join them. Several weeks after the incident at church they met with more than the usual crowd. It was obvious that The Reverend Bradley Goodman was in charge at this weekly breakfast gathering at Matty's Diner. The preacher was talking about the shameful and disgraceful disturbance Lydia had caused in his church. He went on to say that she must be under the influence of Satan since she had stopped going to church on Sundays. He was still talking as he raised his cup to Matty as a signal that he wanted a refill. She did not pick up the coffee pot. Instead she went over to the table where he was still talking a little too loud to suit her about Lydia and her sinful ways. "Gentlemen," she said as she gathered up their half eaten breakfast, "Since you have finished I suggest that you carry your conversation about my very good friend outside."

The reverend scrapped back his chair threw his napkin on the table and stomped out with Leroy followed on his heels. This time he did not leave a tip. Some of the other members of the group smiled sheepishly at Matty before they left.

Leroy evidently had not told the reverend that Lydia had decided to attend services at Windfield First Church in town where she and Aunt Ruth had attended. Every Sunday Leroy made every attempt to make her late. The old crowd was gone now and it did not feel like home anymore but she was not about to let Leroy know how this made her feel. He told her that she needed go to church with him and that she had been forgiven after she apologized for disturbing the service when she stood to speak.

Chapter 12

Leroy dropped down in the pink vinyl covered glider and unlaced his well worn farm boots as he did each afternoon. Heaving a heavy sigh he pulled at the steel-toed shoe and let it drop causing Lydia to jump.

I don't know why I do this every time. I should know by now what is coming. If he would just admit that his feet have grown and buy larger boots he would not have so much trouble getting them off.

Lydia frowned as she spooned the mashed potatoes into the serving dish. *Darn, I wish he'd leave those dirty boots outside on the porch. He leaves little clumps of mud wherever he walks. I just hate following in his footsteps cleaning after him every time he comes in. AND I hate that hideous chair. 'MY MA USED TO ROCK ME TO SLEEP IN THIS CHAIR AND I'M GONNA KEEP IT RIGHT HERE. THAT'S THAT AND I DON'T WANT TO HEAR ANOTHER WORD ABOUT IT'"* Lydia shook her head back and forth as she mocked his reply when she wanted to redecorate the room. She so wanted to replace the faded rocker and the old worn out, brown vinyl recliner. It was just so funny she smiled as she repeated to herself her private joke. "The rocker was reserved for yanking off boots. The recliner was for snoring while watching TV."

Lydia looked around at all the things that she had wanted to change to make the house look better. It seemed to her that her life was destined to be lived in this dreary place that did not feel like a home. This room especially was a memorial to Leroy's family and his memories of the "good old days."

The platform rocker was so worn that the tiny pink flowers could be seen only at the edges where the brass colored brads were nailed to the wooden frame. The plastic on the recliner had begun to split in several places from old age and abuse. The splits had been patched with plastic tape which did not cover the hole nor did it stop the splitting. Between the rocker and the recliner was a rough hewn end table covered with nuts, bolts, drill bits, and other odds and ends that found its way into Leroy's pockets. On the other side of the rocker was a match to the other rough hewn end table. On this end table was a reading lamp made of brass. The lamp was Lydia's lone contribution to the "museum'. Behind the rocker sat the 200 pound anvil and the massive hammer that had been used to shape metal horseshoes. These objects had been the object of many a battle over 'what belongs in the barn and what belongs in the house'. *"And I lost each battle!"* muttered Lydia as she slammed the platter of roast beef down on the table. *Another family heirloom* "MY GREAT-GRANDPA USED THIS ANVIL WHEN HE SHOD THE FARM HORSES. AND IT STAYS WHERE IT IS. IT'S TOO HEAVY FOR YOU TO MOVE ANYWAY." *mocking him again with the shake of her head.*

"Just what is wrong with you now? Muttering to yourself and making faces. I guess you're coming to the change of life. That's all I need with everything else." Leroy remarked as he washed his grease and dirt covered hands in the kitchen sink and dried them on the clean dish cloth that Lydia had just put out.

"Just one more thing to tick me off," thought Lydia as she sat down to the meal. She did not hear the blessing Leroy gave because she was still thinking of all the things that was going wrong in her life. There seemed to be nothing she could do to please Leroy and heaven knows **SHE** was not pleased.

"Lord help me to know your will. I just don't know what to do. Leroy keeps quoting scripture or what he says is in the <u>Bible</u>. I have always tried to do what I thought You want me to do. But lately it is so hard to know what to do. Forgive me for doubting but I just don't feel that You want me to be a doormat for Leroy. You gave me an inquisitive mind and the love of mechanics and the ability to reason things out and to discover how things work. Leroy

doesn't understand that I like to take things apart to see how they work even though I put them back together. He calls this childish play. Lord I need your help .Amen"

As Lydia ate her eyes were drawn to the *"memorial wall"* just beyond the *family heirlooms*. There on the wall were old and rusted farm items that too belonged in a barn: a crosscut saw, cotton scales with the weights, several plow heads, horse shoes, and a bee smoker.

"I try to keep in mind because I have heard so many times the clichés that "a man's home is his castle". But I have heard so many others as well: you can attract bees with honey not vinegar, a little bit of honey makes the medicine go down just to name a few. But a little voice in my head calls to memory another trite saying, 'if you don't lie down no one can step on you.' I am also constantly reminded from the pulpit and Sunday School lessons that a woman's place is in the home, the husband is head of the household, women are subservient to men, and a woman should not have dominance over a man, blah, blah, blah. However, that little voice again (some may say the devil is sneaking up on me) says "Then why did God give me a brain? If He wanted me to be docile why not make me an idiot, one who cannot think but can only follow orders."

As she ate without tasting Lydia prayed, *"Lord, I need help in knowing just what you want of me. I do so want to do Your will but it is so hard to understand. Is it because, as Leroy says, that I am trying to make myself more important than I am. He says that in the <u>Bible</u> this is a sin. Lord, when I read Your word I just don't get that impression. I get the feeling that You are a God of love as well as a disciplinarian. I just nee….."*

"LYDIA, WHAT HAS GOTTEN INTO YOU LATELY?' Leroy exclaimed loudly then lowered his voice when she dropped her fork as she jumped. She turned from her prayer back into reality.

"Didn't you hear me? I need another glass of tea and my glass didn't have enough ice in it. I've notice lately that you are having trouble with your hearing on top of everything else. Is something wrong with you? Maybe you need to go see Dr. Lucas. I want you to call tomorrow and make an appointment."

Chapter 13

THE NEXT TUESDAY AT THE regular breakfast get-together Leroy commented about Lydia's "odd behavior". Preacher Goodman suggested a visit to Dr. Jonas Meuller may be in order. He went on to explain that he had referred several of his parishioners to him.

"Lord knows she needs something." Leroy exclaimed. "I don't have time for her moods just when I need to get hay baled and out of the field. With rain in the forecast and my mower on the fritz I don't need anything else to worry about."

After he got home Leroy mulled over the good reverend's suggestion and decided to give Dr. Meuller a call. After telling him about how nervous Lydia seemed to be of late, they decided that the doctor would drop in for a "friendly visit and take a look" at her.

On the appointed day of Dr. Mueller's visit, Lydia had promised to make a change in Alice's display. She had new beauty supplies to come in and wanted to show them in the window. It was just after 7 AM and Leroy was still in the house which was unusual. Lydia had expected him to already be headed out to work on something or go to the store for supplies. He seemed to be looking for something and continued to look out the window.

Lydia ignored him as she finished the breakfast dishes and cleaned the bathroom. With breakfast over she had just enough time to go set up the display and return to prepare dinner by 12 noon. She usually did not leave until Leroy was out. He kept showing her things that needed to be done.

"Here's a dirty cup you missed. And I noticed that the coffee tasted funny this morning like the pot needs to be washed."

"Where did you find that cup? I know I looked around to see if you carried a cup with you. But you kept moving around and looking out the window. Are you expecting someone?"

Leroy didn't answer but turned around as if he didn't hear her.

After tidying a little more she decided to go anyway. She changed into jeans and a white oversized cotton shirt, put a little color on her lips, and ran a brush through her hair. Leroy did not like for her to go out wearing jeans but they were comfortable to work in as she did display work. He had agreed for Lydia to do this work for Alice when she told him that Alice would swap haircuts for her work. It was hard for her to answer to his demands but he kept reminding her that the <u>Bible</u> said that the man should be head of the household. And the head of the household was responsible for those under his roof. She looked around to see if there was anything else that Leroy could find to delay her. Finding none she headed out.

Lydia opened the door to leave and jumped back because a man had his hand raised to knock. Leroy pushed past Lydia and reached for Dr. Meuller's hand. "Come in, come in" he said as he shook his hand and pulled him into the room. "Lydia, this is D uh Jonas a friend of mine. Why don't you fix us a cup of coffee? We'll just sit and visit for awhile." Leroy followed with his hand on her back as he ushered her into the kitchen area. "I know Jonas and you will just get along fine."

"What do you mean?" whispered Lydia with a shocked look on her face. "Who is he and why is he here now? I don't have time to visit with a stranger. I promised Alice I would be at the beauty shop at 8:30 .I don't like to be late. Alice wants me to set up a new display because a shipment of new line of supplies has just come in and she wants to display them. I need to finish up there and be back in time to make lunch. You know how you are about your sensitive stomach."

"Oh for goodness sake Lydia, it won't hurt to be a little late to visit with a friend of mine. You can play with your toy trains anytime. Why don't you fix us a cup of coffee and come sit. We'll have a nice visit with D uh, uh, Jonas."

"Well, this is new. Where did that come from? He's actually asking **ME** to sit and talk with a friend of his? Okay God, help me get through this without raising my blood pressure. I really need to get to Alice's shop and get back home to cook lunch. You know how upset Leroy gets when a meal is late .I can do without his tirades right now."

"You want me to fix a pot of coffee in that dirty pot?"

Leroy ignored her and went in to sit with Dr. Mueller.

Lydia did go in with a tray of coffee and sat down. As they talked she thought Jonas asked her a lot of mindless questions but she thought she would endure the visit a little longer then she will just have to go.

"Leroy, I just have to go. Alice needs the display set up today. As it is I may be late getting lunch ready. It was nice meeting you Mr. uh …D. Jonas. I am sorry to cut my visit with you but I know you and Leroy have lots to catch up on. And I will just be in the way."

Lydia saw the disapproving look on Leroy's face as she left.

As she rushed into the beauty shop out of breath and apologizing about being late, Alice slowed her down. "It's alright. Sit down and take a breath. You are never late. So tell me what's going on."

"I just don't know what Leroy was doing but he had a friend over. First of all he always leaves the house just after breakfast. This morning he kept hanging around and looking out the window. Then as I was going out the door a friend of his showed up. As if that wasn't enough of a surprise, he invited me to sit and visit with his friend. I have never heard Leroy speak of this friend. AND this friend talked to me more than to Leroy. It was so weird. He kept asking such silly questions. Like, 'How do you feel about this? How does it make you feel when you put your small trains together?' I tell you the truth I just didn't like him that much. He gave me the willies".

Lydia stood up and looked around at the products that Alice wanted displayed and began to plan how to set up the window.

"Well so much for that. I can enjoy myself for an hour or two. I did tell Leroy I may be late with supper. I tell you the truth I just don't know how much more I can take. He makes me so mad…"

She stopped and put her handover her mouth when she noticed that her voice was louder than usual. She had not shared her frustration about

Leroy before. She also noticed that the others in the shop had stopped talking and realized that they must have overheard what she said.

"I'm terribly sorry ladies. I didn't mean to disturb you. I'm just frustrated because Leroy made me late."

Some of the women waved her off with, "That's okay we all been there."

The women started talking again but not back to usual din. The conversations were hushed and they turned away from Lydia.

"Don't give it another thought."Alice said as she gave her a little hug and whispered, "These ladies could use something new to talk about other than whose perm needs more curl and who uses too much eye shadow. But just so you know the biggest gossips are in here today. So don't be surprised if you get some more odd questions from our good citizens. I just hope Leroy doesn't take it the wrong way."

"At this point that is his problem." Lydia whispered back as she held back a tear that threatened to fall, "Even though I promised till death do us part, I am about ready to call it quits."

"You certainly are in need of a talk and a drink. Slip out this evening after supper and meet me at Denny's grill. I am not taking no for an answer." Alice said as she returned to her customers.

After Lydia left, Leroy asked Dr. Meuller "Well, what do you think?"

"You are right. Your wife certainly needs some help. She seems to be on the verge of a nervous breakdown. She could not sit still. It was as if she were on pins the way she kept squirming around. She also seemed to be obsessed with time the way she kept looking at her watch. She also kept wringing her hands. You say she plays with toys? That isn't a good sign either. When do you think you can convince her to come for a formal visit?"

"That may take some doing. She does have a stubborn streak when it comes to the window displays and playing with her toys. This has been going on for years. As a matter of fact even before we were married she did what she called 'work' with toys. I am afraid it will take some extensive therapy to overcome that."

Lydia was in a bad state when she met Alice at Denny's. She was visibly shaken and red eyed from holding back tears.

Alice rushed to her and led her to a booth in the back. "What in the world happened? Are you okay?"

There had been a stormy confrontation before she left the house.

After supper dishes were washed and the kitchen cleaned, Lydia told Leroy that she was going back to town.

"What do you need in town this late? There's nothing open."

"I'm going to meet a friend."

"A friend? What's HIS name?"

"Oh for goodness sakes Leroy, I am just meeting Alice. I need to get out once in a while."

'It's not decent for a woman to go out at this time of night, Even if you are meeting with Alice. And Alice? She's no friend she just wants you to continue playing in the window with her beauty stuff so she can make a sale."

"I'll be back in a while." Lydia said as she slung her purse over her shoulder."

"Damn it woman, you don't need to go out this late. What will people say? Besides that you might have a wreck driving at night. And that rattletrap isn't driving right. Even I had a hard time keeping it going. It could stop on you right in the middle of the road."

"Leroy, I know how to drive. I have been driving a long time. I was driving before I met you." Lydia was getting angry at this point.

"It's okay for me to drive that big 6 wheel diesel truck when you want me to go pick up something for the farm. Now you don't think I can drive a small car."

She didn't seem to be able to stop once she got started, "And if you don't want me to drive 'that old rattletrap', why did you insist that it was fine for me to drive when you wanted to swap your old truck, which by the way was younger than my car, for a newer truck. I needed a better car more than you needed another truck." She was so hurt and angry that she started to cry, which made her even angrier.

"Lydia, what in hell is wrong with you to defy me this way?" yelled Leroy as he advanced toward her with raised fists. His face was flushed and he was gritting his teeth "Who have you been talking with to go against me like this? And you can turn of the waterworks. That may work on other people but it won't work on me."

Lydia backed away and ran out the door.

"I really think he was going to hit me." She told Alice later. "I don't know what will happen when I go back home."

After Lydia told Alice about the argument, it took about an hour for her nerves to settle down.

"How long has this been going on? You never said a thing before. I have noticed though that you haven't been your usual cheerful self for a long time. I just didn't want to meddle in your business because I know you are a private person and keep worries to yourself."

"I don't like airing my problems. I'm so sorry about this but Leroy made me so angry. I have prayed and prayed asking God to tell me what to do, to show me the way to handle this. But He hasn't answered me yet. Or I didn't recognize the answer. It may have been 'stick with it.' "

She sighed, "When I tried to get away for a respite there was always something that came up."

They sat talking quietly until Molly came over and told them that Asa was closing.

Leroy was already in bed when she returned so Lydia went into the spare bedroom, slipped off her dress and slid between the sheets. She was so exhausted she went right to sleep.

The next morning she was up first and had breakfast on the table when Leroy came in and sat down to eat. Nothing was said about the night before.

Chapter 14

Lydia was finishing the breakfast dishes when Leroy put down a magazine he had been reading.

"Lydia, according to the Farmer's Almanac here, the moon is in the right phase to start planting the garden. So I want you to go to Brown's Farm and Garden today and pick up the seeds that we usually get. Now don't you let Sammy talk you into any of the new hybrid stuff either? The store hasn't been the same since Dan sold it to Sammy. Dan always knew what I wanted. Oh yes, get a 50 lb bag of 10-10-10." Leroy refused to acknowledge that it was no longer Browns but Evans Feed and Seed.

While you're gone I'll get out the tractor and plow the garden spot and lay off the rows. By the way, I may be going out later. If I'm not back you can start with the green beans on the far side.

Lydia cleared her throat "You know, I've been thinking about planting the rows closer together this year and putting grass clippings between the rows to keep the weeds down. That way the garden won't need to be hoed so much.'

Leroy whirled around and glared at her, "What do you mean you've been thinking? A garden needs to be hoed."

'Yes, but this way it won't take up as much space."

'I will lay out the rows as I usually do to give the vegetables space to grow and that's that."

DANGEROUS OCCUPATION

"But when the vegetables get ripe, it's so hard to keep up with picking, canning, and weeding at the same time. I really get tired with all the work. Then, by midsummer weeds take over".

"Oh for goodness sake Lydia stop your nagging. I don't want to hear any more of your ideas." He stalked off muttering to himself, "I don't know where she gets these hair brained ideas of hers." Then he yelled over his shoulder, "Don't take too long in town. It'll get dark before you know it."

"Hello Miss Lydia," smiled Sammy when she entered the feed and seed store. "It is always good to see you."

"And a good morning to you too Sammy. How are Missy and the twins?"

"They are just fine, growing like weeds, the children that is. Boy, I had better not say that around Missy. She is so sensitive about her weight these days. She has been so busy helping me out here and … Oh yeah, you may not have heard. Missy is helping out at *The Shiphrah House*. She told me about how her family was helped out when her brother-in-law got hurt. She said that she knew somehow your Aunt Ruth had something to do with it and wanted to return the favor by working there."

Lydia didn't acknowledge that he was right, "That's great! They sure could use a hand there and Missy grew up to be a sweet and caring person. Tell her hello for me. Now I had better finish up here. Leroy is waiting for me to return and 'Don't give me any of that newfangled stuff', she laughed as she quoted Leroy.

"I know Miss Lydia. I have tried to get Leroy to just try out some new seeds that we have but he wants 'what Dan always sold me'," he laughed as he quoted Leroy too.

When she returned Lydia was going to plead her case again. She felt it was safe to try again. Not long after an argument Leroy usually acted as if nothing had happened. It was as if he had made a ruling and all was settled. But she could not find him. She looked in the garage. Her old Chevy was gone.

"Well, I had to go to the seed store and get supplies. But he couldn't bother because he had more important things to do. The garden hasn't been plowed either. Now I have to unload the fertilizer myself. It was nice of Sammy to load it for me. He is such a polite young man. I am glad that he and Melissa got together. They seem to be such a happy family."

She unloaded the truck as she prayed, "*Lord, how do I go about getting Leroy to understand how I feel without causing him to get so angry?*"

After the evening meal she tried again, "I was reading in Mother Earth that it is a good idea to mulch between rows to keep down weeds and garden pests. It said that shredded newspapers were good mulch. Why don't we try that?"

"The garden needs to be worked to loosen the soil between the rows to allow the roots of the vegetables to get air. That's why it needs to be hoed." He explained to Lydia as if he were instructing a child.

Planting went as Leroy had decided. He plowed the garden with his 5610 John Deere. Then Lydia and Leroy made shallow ditches by dragging a hoe in the soft soil. This was done in rows 3 feet apart.

Then he continued with his instructions, "We'll plant three rows of sweet corn on the left edge of the garden. Then we need two rows of okra, three rows of green beans, one row of cayenne and jalapeño peppers, two rows of tomatoes, two rows of butterbeans, one row of bell peppers, one row of butter peas, and one row of radishes. You need to get the tomato plants tomorrow before the soil dries out."

The next day, Lydia found herself the sole planter of the garden. She jumped as a clap of thunder sounded close. "*Lord, give me a little while longer. I need to get the tomatoes set out before it rains. The clouds are so dark it may start to pour just any minute.*"

Two weeks later Leroy sat in the rocker to put on his boots, "The weeds are taking over garden again. Remember how you complained that the heat sapped your energy. You need to get out there before the sun gets too hot. I have to go help Joe load a few cows to carry to the sale. Maybe I can help if I get back before the sun goes down."

Since he did not seem to be angry Lydia felt it was okay to suggest another solution. "There was an ad in Mother Earth showing a garden tiller. Maybe we can buy one to till between the rows. I could use it to plow up most of the weeds. Then it won't be so hard to keep the garden clean."

"Damn it woman are you still on that kick? What makes you think you can handle a tiller? A city girl like you knows nothing about farm equipment. You might hurt yourself. I don't have time to carry you to the doctor after you break your fool neck. Would you give me a break and stop nagging?"

Leroy turned as he was going out the door, "You know that the Bible says, *A nagging woman is like the constant dripping of rain.* That's called Chinese torture."

Lydia knew when there was no use trying to talk. So she let the subject drop.

"Well, I can certainly handle a 3/4 ton duely when Leroy needs something from the feed store. I can heft a 50 lb bag of fertilizer when he isn't around. I can dig in the hard ground when the garden needs weeding. But I can't handle a machine that will make my work load easier."

"Darn, I just hate it when this happens", muttered Lydia when a clod of dirt flipped over and filled her shoes as she chopped the weeds in the garden. She could hear Leroy's comment still, "Lydia, the weeds are taking over the vegetables. You'll have to use a sling blade to get around in there if you let it go any longer."

"Why is it always the woman who is expected to get rid of the weeds, a woman who knows nothing about gardening? Well, where does he think the vegetables came from that Aunt Ruth and I canned each year? I used to enjoy working in the garden with Aunt Ruth. Why does it seem to be such a chore now? Am I getting to be a constant nag like Leroy suggests? "

"Lord." Lydia prayed, *"I really don't want to turn into an old nag. I just can't talk with anyone but You about my feelings about Leroy and how he puts me down"*

It seemed to Lydia that every time she gets to a point of exacerbation with Leroy a sermon or Sunday School lesson centers around the duties of the wife and how she is to be submissive to her husband. *"Lord is that You answering my prayers about how to deal with my husband's actions and words?"*

Lydia's face lit up as she scanned the mail that afternoon. A letter had come from Kate, her best friend in the world. It had been such a long time since she had gone to see her in Minnesota.

"Look what just came." Lydia waved the letter excitedly at Leroy. She was so excited that she needed to tell someone and Leroy was the only one at hand.

"What, another issue of Mother Earth? I could do without anymore advice from that source of crap."

Immediately Lydia's face dropped. "No it's a letter from Kay. It has been such a long time since I have talked with her. I can't wait to read what she has to say".

Lydia wanted to rush to her bedroom to read the letter alone where she could savor her friend's words. They always brought a happy feeling to her gloomy world. And heaven knows she needed a kind word these days.

Kate's letter was full of news about the family. It was such a blessing to hear such a full and happy life that Kate was living. Lydia reread it several times because it made her feel so uplifted after her confrontation with Leroy. The part that made her heart skip a beat was the invitation to visit.

"Dee, it has been such a long time since you have visited. I miss you so much. Our short talks over the phone just aren't enough. The last time you visited was when Ruthie was 2 and Jamie was just born." Can you believe that was nine years ago? Lydia, I want to see you face to face. Don't take this the wrong way but I am worried about you. The last time I talked with you I felt that something is wrong. The last few years you haven't sounded like yourself. I know you have a tendency to keep things to yourself.

Remember that time in 8th grade you were so worried about your Aunt Ruth that you got sick and threw up in class? When Aunt Ruth came after you I was allowed to go home with you. It took us both a while to get you to open up and tell us what was wrong. It turned out that Aunt Ruth was just busy with the Shiphrah House where young mothers who could not care for their babies could come and get the help needed. This had been on her mind for a long time and she was trying to find a way to help.

You take after Aunt Ruth in that way. I remember how you took Missy under your wing when she needed a friend after her uncle Jules had that bad accident and could not work.

I don't want you getting sick way out there where I can't take over for Aunt Ruth and pester you to tell me what is wrong.

I could be wrong since it has been so long and maybe I am reading signs that aren't there. I want you to come out here and let me see for myself.

I am sending this ticket that is nonrefundable. I am not taking no for an answer. I want to see you. I could come there but I have my reasons for not doing that at this time. But I will if you don't come here."

Lydia knew the reason. By his actions even before they married Leroy showed that he did not like Kate or Samuel, her husband. He had told Lydia that they thought they were better than she was and that they were just putting on a show.

"Lydia!" yelled Leroy, "What in the world does that snob Kate say that's keeping you from cooking supper? I need to eat soon. You know what the doctor said about my sensitive stomach."

Lydia didn't want to spoil her excitement by arguing with Leroy, so she hurriedly put the letter in her lingerie drawer. And went out to "Do her duty as a wife."

"Well, what did she have to say? It must have been a lot, it took you long enough."

Lydia had had enough and decided to let him have it with both barrels, "Okay, here it is. She sent me a ticket to come visit her and I am going."

"She what?" sputtered Leroy. "I told you she thought she was better that you. Does she think I can't take care of my own family?"

Lydia ignored the comment and went into the kitchen.

Leroy tried another tactic. "Anyway the garden will be coming in and it'd be a shame to let all your hard work go to waste. It would be better if you go in September. By then the vegetables will be giving out and your canning will be finished. I know how much you enjoy the canning of your fresh vegetables. They are so much better than the canned ones from the grocery store. September will be much better. You can swap the ticket for then since it's already been paid for."

As if the decision had been settled, he reached for his hat. "Call me on my cell when supper is ready."

Lydia turned around and starred him in the eye and calmly said."I am not waiting until September. I am going this week, the date that's on the ticket."

He stomped around the room for awhile and threw his hat on the floor. He was taken aback. Lydia had never talked to him in that tone before. She was getting out of hand and he didn't like it one little bit. That's when he totally lost his temper.

He yanked a picture of Kate, Samuel, Ruthie, and Jamie off the wall and threw it down. The glass shattered over the floor as Lydia watched in a panic. "You are not going!"

By this time Lydia was numb. She surprised herself as she calmly spoke to Leroy, "Yes I am going. AND tonight you can get your own supper." She turned and went to their bedroom where she got a few clothes, a blanket and toiletries and went into the spare bedroom. Leroy was livid as he stomped out of the house and headed for town. After he left Lydia went back into the bedroom and packed her bags for the trip.

Leroy slid into a booth at Denny's and looked at the menu.

"My gracious Leroy, you look like you are about to bust a gut" Molly grinned as she pulled her pad out of her little apron and prepared to take his order, "This is a first for you. What brings you here at this time of day? Don't Lydia usually cook supper for you?"

That brought such an angry scowl that Molly shut her mouth and turned her skimpy clad self around and fled back to the counter where she pretended to be busy.

"Ain't you going to wait on Leroy?' asked Asa, the cook.

Molly shook her head, "Since he's the only customer here, you can see what he wants. AND I suggest you don't ask any questions if you would like for your head to stay on your shoulders."

Then she added as if to herself, "We sure have had our fill of Martins this month. Just the other day Lydia was in here with Alice. They were talking in whispers and Lydia's eyes all red from crying. But she looked like she could bite a ten penny nail into. Now, Leroy stomps in here with his head up his butt."

Asa slid in the booth across from Leroy, "What can I fry up for you Leroy? You look like you could use a juicy steak. Or do you need a piece of humble pie. From the looks of Lydia the other day, you might try that."

"Asa, you know what you can do with your advice. Bring me that steak and make it rare. And for your information Lydia has been in a snit these days. Why don't you both mind your own damn business. And you can tell that to Miss short skirt over there as well." He pointed his chin in Molly's direction.

"Boy that must have been a doosey of a fight they had," Commented Molly after Leroy left.

Chapter 15

Sophie Pearson tapped on the door of Lydia's hospital room. It had been over two weeks since Leroy was killed and Lydia was rendered unconscious. "Lydia, good I see you are awake. My, it is so good to see you. You are looking a lot better than when I saw you last. Two weeks in a coma, I guess you know how worried everyone has been."

Just then Alice Young came in, "Thank God, you're awake." She went over and kissed Lydia on the cheek then wiped off the lipstick with her fingers. "Hi, Sophie, how's the real estate business going? Would you just look at the pretty flowers?" She went over and looked at the cards, "Here's one from Jules and Jan Gordon, Sammy and Melissa Evans, and…"

"My real estate business is doing fine, Alice. How is the beautician business?"

"Great. By the way Lydia I heard that Sheriff Williams was in here yesterday. How did that go? There are all kinds of rumors going around. Everyone seems to have an opinion as to what happened to Leroy. Did the sheriff tell you anything?" Alice had a way of asking questions without giving anyone a chance to answer. "Oh, and I heard that he put out an APB out for that person who's been breaking into homes around here."

Sophie tried to change the subject, "Sammy and his friends have been looking after your farm animals."

When Alice got started it was hard to stop her, "AND Preacher

DANGEROUS OCCUPATION

Goodman keeps going on about what a good Christian man Leroy was and it is such a shame he had to die so young. When he was in Matty's Diner Tuesday he made Matty so mad she made him leave because she overheard him say what a hard life he had putting up with your antics.

"Alice!" yelled Sophie.

"Well, that's what I heard. I am so sorry, Lydia, sometimes my mouth opens before my brain kicks in."

There was a knock on the hospital door and a tall trim man walked in. He was standing so straight it made him appear taller. He was wearing a freshly pressed khaki uniform with creases so sharp it looked as if it was pressed by someone in the military.

"Mrs. Martin, remember me? I'm Sheriff Chester McCormick I was in here yesterday. How are you today?"

"Yes sheriff I remember. These are friends Alice and Sophie."

"Ladies," he gave a small nod. "I have seen them around town. Lydia, I need to continue where I left off yesterday. I hope your memory is better today. Since you have company I'll come back later. Shall we say in about an hour? It was nice to see you Ladies again."

Alice looked worried, "Lydia, since the sheriff is asking you questions, and all the rumors going around, have you thought about getting a lawyer?"

"What...what?" Lydia was stunned, "What in the world do you mean?" Lydia looked around wildly, "I, I, I don't know why I would need a lawyer."

"Alice!" Sophie yelled again. "For goodness sake can't you see how upset Lydia is? I can't believe you would do such a thing"

"Think about it Sophie. When a person is murdered, who is the first person the police suspect? The spouse."

"Alice, you watch too much TV."

"Murdered? Do they think Leroy was murdered? I don't know why anyone would murder Leroy."

"What should I do Sophie? Do you think I should? Oh dear, I shouldn't put you in that position. I don't know who I could call for advice, certainly not Preacher Goodman. I'm just not thinking clearly."

Just then Dr. Matthews walked in as usual this time of day checking on his patients. He had heard the last of the conversation, "If you pardon my intrusion, I couldn't help but overhear. Mrs. Martin, you have a skull fracture and aren't as clear headed as you usually are. You are a very intelligent woman but at this point you probably do need someone to help you as you answer the sheriff's questions. I know this isn't my place to say but I am speaking as a friend not as your doctor. What harm could it do?"

"I don't know, wouldn't that make me appear to have something to hide? Yet I am so confused maybe I do need someone who is thinking clearer than I am at this time."

When the sheriff returned he found Lydia quite upset from what Alice had told her. "I was afraid of that. That's why I wanted to talk with you so soon. Remember I said that I wanted to ask you questions while it was fresh on your mind."

"Is it true that you have reason to believe that Leroy was murdered?"

"We can't rule it out. We are still looking into all possibilities. I understand that you may want a lawyer present."

"Sheriff, I don't really know if I need one but I'm afraid that I may not be able to answer your questions without someone helping me sort them out. Do you think I need one?"

"Now I can't advise you on that seeing as I am the one who will be questioning you. But if you would feel better then by all means call your lawyer. I just need to get this done as quickly as possible the sooner the better."

"Thank you. The only lawyer I know is Felix Fields, the one Leroy calls when he needs legal matters handled. I can't think of anyone else to call right now. I guess I could call him. I just hope this doesn't make me appear guilty of something."

It was 6 o'clock, after business hours, before Felix found the time to be at the questioning. When he entered the hospital room, introductions were made and he took a seat off to the side. "I have already been briefed on the reason for this interview. So you can proceed with the questioning and I will interrupt if I need to. Mrs. Martin feel free to stop and ask questions before you answer." At this he sat back, crossed his arms and leaned his chair against the wall as if to say, *"Okay I have performed my duty as her attorney"*.

While they were waiting for Felix she had been trying to remember what had happened. Since she had just learned about Leroy's death, she was very confused.

"Now Lydia," the sheriff said as he placed the recorder on the hospital tray near her, "I want you to go back to June 28th can you tell me what happened?"

"I've been trying to figure that out myself. Ok, where do I begin? Let's see, earlier that morning I gathered vegetables from the garden. I was cooking them for dinner, okra, squash, and green beans, cornbread and a beef roast, and iced tea, Leroy's favorite meal. I went to the bathroom while Leroy took off his work boots as he usually does when he comes in to eat. He doesn't like to wear them too long because they pinch his feet and the steel toes make them so heavy. I tried to tell him that people's feet continue to grow after adulthood and his shoes were probably too small. But he blamed the pinching on the steel toes."

Lydia had to laugh when she thought of his routine. It had always been so funny to her. When everyone in the room looked at her with puzzlement she explained.

"Leroy always took his work boots off as he sat in his 'mama's rocker.' Then he changed over to sit in the recliner. It never made any sense to me. I just thought it was so funny."

"Anyway, as I was saying we were getting ready to eat dinner or it may be lunch to you. The table was already set and I started back from the bathroom to put the food on the table. Leroy likes to eat at 12 noon so it must have been about that time. This is where it gets confusing. I think I heard a loud crash. And I think something hit me in the head, I'm not too sure about that. I just don't remember anything else. The next thing I knew Nurse Grace was calling my name and I had tremendous head ache. That's it. I don't remember anything else until I woke up here. I don't remember anything, absolutely nothing until Nurse Grace spoke to me here in the hospital. Lydia fell back on the pillow exhausted.

"That will be enough for today." Grace said after the monitor at the nurse's station went off. "Dr. Matthews left strict orders that Lydia was not to be questioned after she grew overly tired. A patient with a concussion doesn't think clearly, anyway"

When the sheriff started to ask another question, Grace repeated that this was DOCTOR'S ORDERS. She wondered why Lawyer Fields had not called a halt to the questioning before now since it was clear that Lydia was tired and confused.

The sheriff turned off the recorder and prepared to leave as he neared the door he turned back, "I'll be talking with you again. In a few days you may start to remember more. I do want to remind you though not to leave the county. Good evening Mrs. Martin."

"That reminds me Sheriff. What did you mean when you said yesterday 'Otherwise I will have to send a police escort with you to insure that you won't escape before we have a chance to find out just what happened.' What was that all about?"

"Oh, that was just my sorry excuse for a joke."

He turned around and hit his head with the ball of his hand, "I am so sorry Lydia, uh Mrs. Martin, where are my manners? I just hate that I missed Leroy's funeral. It happened so fast that it was over with before I found out about it."

"Leroy has already been buried? How could that happen?" Lydia was so shocked she couldn't think of anything else to say.

"Why yes, as soon as the coroner released the body, Rev. Goodman arranged for it to be picked up by the funeral home. The reverend is such a slick talker I am sure he had the funeral director convinced that that is what you would want. I am truly sorry Mrs. Martin."

As he left he met the reverend coming in "Reverend," he spoke and continued out. "That poor woman." He said to himself.

"Miss Lydia I came as soon as I heard that you had awakened. I am so sorry for your loss.

"Oh, yes and I heard that you have been busy what with burials and such." Lydia's sarcasm went right over his head.

He went on without missing a beat, "You don't have to thank me Miss Lydia. I am just a servant of the Lord and I'm willing to step in wherever there is a need. Since you were indisposed so to speak, I did what Leroy would have wanted. He is buried near his mother. I am sure that is what he would have wanted. Leroy was such a good man, would give anyone he shirt off his back. Now some punk had to go and kill him."

Just then the monitor at the nurses' station indicated that there was a problem with Lydia.

Nurse Grace rushed in, "You will have to leave now Rev. Goodman. As I told you before, Lydia needs her rest." She took his arm and ushered him out of the room with him sputtering about his being her preacher, her comforter, her counselor.

"I am so sorry. I tried to dissuade him but…"

"Don't worry about it," Lydia broke in, "I know what a bulldozer he is. He can make me so mad sometimes with his arrogance. But he probably is right that Leroy would want to be buried near his mama. This has been such a day. I am totally wiped out and as you say, 'need my rest'."

"By the way, why was that deputy outside my door yesterday?"

"Oh, that was just Cliff. He works here part time when the sheriff doesn't need him. He's harmless. He just likes to nose around. He lives alone and I guess he has nothing better to do." She didn't bother to tell Lydia that the sheriff had left strict orders that no one, especially Alice, was to be allowed to tell Lydia anything else about the case. "I don't want anything said to influence what she tells me about what happened."

The next morning when the sheriff came in there was nothing new Lydia could think of to tell him. It was the same as she had told him before. She was getting dinner for them. Leroy was taking off his boots. She went to the bathroom. Some noise and something hit her in the head.

"Dr. Matthews told me this morning that I could go home today. Sophie and Alice said that they could take time staying with me until I get on my feet. It sure will be good to sleep in my own bed and get out of these hospital gowns. I know I must look a sight. Alice brought me some makeup but I sure will be glad to have my own lipstick. I don't have anything, my purse, my cell phone."

"I'm afraid you can't do that right now Mrs. Martin. Your house is a crime scene. Your farm has been blocked off and no one is allowed in there except me, the coroner, and my deputies. Well, I do let Sammy Evans go in to see to your animals after the barn had been checked out. I have arranged to have you stay in a bed and breakfast in town. You won't even have to cook for yourself. I'll bring you your purse and cell phone.

Deputy Crane said that there was a suitcase in the spare bedroom packed with women's clothes. I could arrange to have it brought to you. Were you planning on a trip?"

"Oh my goodness, Kay, what day is it? Kay must be frantic. I should be in Minnesota right now."

"Yes, we did find your flight plans. The ticket, I'm afraid, has expired."

"They went through my house, my things. No wonder he told me to stay close by. What are they looking for that takes so long?"

"You went through everything in my house! You even went through purse, my personal items! Do you know how that makes me feel? I feel naked. I'm sorry to be so blunt but that is just how I feel. No wonder it took you so long. My house must be a mess. What in the world are you looking for anyway?"

"Now Mrs. Martin, don't get upset. We just want to make sure that we don't miss anything that may be important. You never know what will be imperative in a case like this. And before you think of it you don't have to worry about your house. I personally made sure everything was left as it was except for the few items we took and those were catalogued.

"As for the plane ticket, SHERIFF," Lydia was beginning to lose her temper, "my friend Kay sent it to me! She wanted me to visit. It has been a long time since we have seen each other so she sent the ticket to insure that I come. THAT also explains the packed bags too!"

When the deputy brought her cell phone, the first person she called was Kate. "Dee, where are you? I have been worried out of my mind. I kept calling with no answer. Then your answering machine was full."

When Lydia told her all the things that had happened, Kate insisted that she would be on a plane as soon as she could arrange it.

Chapter 16

Sheriff McCormick and Lydia were sitting in the parlor drinking tea. The sheriff had not come to question Lydia this time. She had requested this meeting.

"Sheriff, when can I go back home? I've been here in this bed and breakfast over a week now and I am well enough to stay by myself. Surly you have finished checking out my house by now. It's been three weeks counting the two weeks I was unconscious. Have you learned anything? What happened? How did Leroy die? I have been patient all this time. I have told you all I know and I feel that it is time for you to let me know what you have discovered so far."

"Well Lydia, uh Mrs. Martin I guess you are right."

"Lydia is fine," she interrupted, "I think by now we have known each other long enough to be on a first name basis."

"And I am tired of being known only as The Sheriff. So you can call me Chess, short for Chester. We have done a thorough search of the house, took fingerprints, and outlined the bod- ... well never mind about that. I just can't see any way this could have been an accident. The autopsy showed that he died of a blow to the head. *'There's no reason to tell her that the blow was at the base of his skull.'* So we're calling it a homicide and have questioned everyone that was there that morning."

"Everyone except Phillip Williams, that is. He was the first one there and found you. We talked with his secretary who now works for L.C. Agnew, his replacement. It seems that Phillip had an emergency back at the main office and flew to Chicago after calling 911 and Rev. Goodman. When we matched his time schedule that day and the time of death, he had not left the office at the time. So he could not have done it."

"The insurance agent? My goodness I have forgotten all about him. Leroy did say something about insuring his new farm equipment. I guess I could check on that while I wait here. That will give me something to do."

The sheriff continued, "Rev. Goodman was the next to arrive. His home phone records show that he was at home when Mr. Williams called and had been visiting patients at the hospital before that."

"The Beulah Land Church Care Committee came in after that and they had been visiting at Essie's house when Rev. Goodman called them. So they can vouch for each other."

"Then the paramedics came and later the deputy and I came."

"So you see there is very little to go on. The only plausible suspect at this time is the thief that has been breaking into houses. I hope he hasn't turned to murder now. We have asked people to come forward if they have any information that may help in the investigation. That's all we have so far."

Sheriff McCormick laughed to himself as he went down the steps. *"I can't help laughing when I think of what Deputy Crane said when I suggested that our killer may be a thief* 'My Lord, why would anyone break in someone's house for a bunch of old farm tools?'"

After the sheriff left, Lydia had another visitor. Sammy came by to check on Lydia and to tell her that he was still looking after her animals. "I'm on my there now. It is a hassle just trying to get to the barn though. I sure will be glad when they finish the investigation and take down the police tape."

"So will I Sammy. I have so many things to do. The sheriff just reminded me about insurance and I have to find the policy which must be at home. There's no telling where Leroy put it."

"Sammy, the sheriff thinks someone killed Leroy. They just don't know who. I can't think of anyone who hated him that much. The sheriff seems to thinks that it may be our neighborhood thief. I don't know why a thief would choose our house to rob. We sure don't have anything worth stealing."

It took Sammy longer that he thought to take care of the animals so he thought he would stop by his own house for lunch. When he drove down his driveway he noticed the front door ajar. He had been having trouble with it scrubbing the floor and sometimes not closing completely. *"I remember making sure that the door was shut when I left this morning because Melissa reminded me*, 'That door needs to be fixed, Sammy! I wish they would catch that thief so things can all go back to normal.' *So why is it open now?"*

Sammy parked his truck in the side driveway leading to the barns and took out his shotgun that he had left in the truck. The gun was in the truck because he had heard a pack of coyotes a few nights before. He didn't want to lose another calf to them. He slipped into the house and heard a noise coming from the kitchen. When he stepped in he saw the refrigerator open and a man standing in front of it eating.

"I guess you know that's my lunch you're eating." He said as he pointed the shotgun at him.

The hungry thief whirled around with a cold chicken leg in his mouth.

"Woody," yelled Sammy, "What are you doing?"

Woody swallowed but still held the chicken leg, "Sammy, what are you doing home? I'm sorry but I was so hungry. I knew you and Melissa usually worked at this time and took my chances that you had something to eat. Sammy I am so scared. They think I killed Leroy. I didn't. What am I going to do? I can't go home."

"What makes you say the police think you killed Leroy?"

"I heard on the news that the sheriff was looking for the person who has been breaking into homes as a possible suspect. They don't know it yet, Sammy, but that person is me. I just know it won't be long before they come after me. I'm no murderer Sammy. Okay, okay so I did steal some things but murder, no! You know I wouldn't do that, Sammy. Please help me, Man, please."

"If you are that scared why don't you turn yourself in?"

"Since they already think the one who has been robbing homes is guilty, I'm afraid I will be arrested for murder and convicted before I can prove I didn't do it. Will you go with me? They'll listen to you."

After considering it for awhile Sammy agreed to be with him while he turns himself in. "I hope you know I could be arrested for helping you out. But this is what I will do. I need to go back to the store now. I will think on it for awhile. I'll be back after I close the store. Get something else to eat and some water to drink and go to the barn. Stay there until I return. Do not leave the barn. I'm going to lock the back door of the house and nail the damaged door shut. Now, let me make this very clear, if you are not here when I return I will have you charged with breaking and entering. Is that clear?"

"God Bless you, Man, I WILL be here I promise." He clasped Leroy's hand in both of his.

It was hard for Sammy to concentrate on business that evening so he let his helper do most of the transactions.

He called Melissa on her cell phone, "Melissa I know this is going to sound crazy but I want you to trust me. There is nothing seriously wrong. But there's a small item I have to take care of at home this evening. I want you to just listen and do what I ask and don't ask questions. I will explain later when you come home.

This really set her off, "WHAT? Sammy you ARE SCARING me."

"Stay calm. It has nothing to do with you or me. A friend has asked for my help. And it will take too long for me to explain right now. After work carry the twins and stay at your sister Jan's house until I call you back. Trust me, Honey, and don't worry. It'll be okay."

He then called the sheriff and asked him to meet him at his house after seven o'clock.

"What's this all about? Can't you just tell me what's on your mind over the phone? That's my supper time when I have a chance to eat supper."

"Just trust me Sheriff. It is important. I just can't tell you over the phone. You know me I wouldn't ask this of you if it weren't important."

"Yeah, yeah I know Sammy. This had better be good, at least worth missing supper for."

"Just grab one of your wife's good old homemade biscuits as you leave. That should tide you over," teased Sammy.

"Woody, it's me Sammy," Leroy called when he returned home that evening at 6:30. No one answered. He looked in the barn. He didn't find him there. "Woody, you had better not skip out on me after all I went through for you."

"I'm here Sammy," Woody slipped in from behind the barn. "Just had to relieve myself."

"Okay, this is what I have done so far. Melissa and the twins are staying in town until later this evening. I haven't told anyone a thing. I will leave that up to you. That's why I asked the sheriff to meet me here at seven. Let's go back to the house and we can talk there."

Woody confessed to the burglaries but denied that he had anything to do with killing Leroy.

"You did the right thing turning yourself in. And you do know I have to take you in for breaking and entering. While I'm at it, why shouldn't I charge you with the murder of Leroy?"

"That's why I turned myself in Sheriff. I was scared you would charge me with it. I promise you I didn't do it."

"Well where were you on June 28 of this year?"

"Gosh Sheriff, I don't know. I'll have to think back to remember what was happening at that time."

"Well here's one for you. Leroy was killed that day. Let's go back to jail and I'll let you think on it for a few days."

As soon as the sheriff and Woody left Sammy called to let Melissa know it was safe to return home. When she got there Sammy met her at the car to help with the twins. She grabbed him in a big bear hug. "Thank God you're safe. I have been so worried. What happened? Why did you want me to stay in town? I have been worried sick. I know you told me that everything was okay but that still didn't keep me from thinking about all the possibilities that could be going on. Here you are at home but you tell me to stay away. A friend needed your help but I couldn't come. I kept thinking about the break-ins that have been going on around here. Then I thought about Leroy being killed. How could you think I wouldn't worry?"

"Shh," Sammy put his fingers to her mouth and gave her a squeeze, "Everything is alright. Come on let's get the twins in the house and I will fill you in. It is a story to long to be telling out here in the dark. We'll put the children to bed first."

Melissa was so relieved after hearing all about Sammy's day, "Now I guess you'll have to get that door fixed," she laughed.

Chapter 17

THE DAY AFTER HE WAS arrested Woody was brought into the sheriff's office to be questioned again.

"Okay Woody it's time for us to have a little talk," Sheriff McCormick said as he reared back in his chair and ran his hands through his hair. "I guess you know that you aren't the most popular guy in this county right now. There are a lot of people who would like to have a piece of your hide." He sat forward and leaned his arms on his desk. "I have so many questions for you I don't know where to start," The sheriff was sitting behind his desk in his office. Woody was sitting in front of the desk facing him. Deputy Douglas Crane sat in a chair in the corner.

"I'm going to tape this conversation and I want you to know that anything you say I can use in court against you. You have a right to have a lawyer present. Do you want a lawyer?"

"I don't know a lawyer sheriff. I trust you I've always heard that you are a fair and honest sheriff. But I would feel better if Sammy was here."

"I'm not here to make you feel better but as you say I try to be fair. So I'll give Sammy a call and see if he's willing and has the time to come over. Douglas, would you step out and call Sammy? I have a few things I could be working on while we wait. Woody, take a seat on the bench right outside where I can see you."

The sheriff took a file from the many that were stacked on his unkempt desk. Papers were sticking out of files as if they were hastily shoved into them. He picked up several files and stacked them on another stack so he could open the one he was working on. Behind him were three tall file cabinets along the side wall and two short one under the window. There were folders piled on each cabinet. On top of some were loose papers that needed to be filed. "Lord, I can't finish one case before four more break out. I have so much to do I can't play around holding people's hand because they have heard that they 'should have a lawyer present'." The faded green concrete walls were bare except for a few framed documents and awards. One lone picture of a family was squeezed between a stack of folders under the window.

Sammy came about 20 minutes later and the questioning began. "Woody, tell me about the robberies. I'll just let you start and when you finish I may have some questions. When did you first begin breaking into houses?

"About two years ago I was riding around with some buddies and we saw a bike lying in a yard. One of the guys said it would be easy to just walk over and take it. Later that night I went back to see if I could get away with it. I did. After that it became a game with me to see what I could do without getting caught. It just seemed to take over my life. I just had to try something bigger. A few times I was almost caught but I couldn't stop."

"No excuses, Woody."

"No sir, no excuses I know it is my fault."

"Where did you keep your stash? Who did you sell it to?"

"I didn't sell most of it. I was afraid somebody might recognize their stuff. I stored it in an old shed in back of our house. Mom used to keep garden tools in there until she saw a black widow spider in there. A black snake scared her before that but she's more afraid of black widow spiders than snakes. So she quit going in there. She saw me in there once and I told her I thought I'd clean it out for her. She said that it was real nice of me but to wear gloves and watch out for spiders. So when I went in there I'd carry out some trash and throw it away."

"That's enough for today Woody. Tomorrow we'll go take a look in the shed. Until then I want you to make a list of the houses you visited. Sammy thanks for coming."

DANGEROUS OCCUPATION

"Sheriff," the deputy looked puzzled. "You didn't say a word about Leroy."

"I know. I think I'll let him stew on that for awhile."

The next day they were going over the stolen Items. "This is from the last house." Woody picked up a laptop. I took it from a house over in Greenville County."

Sheriff McCormick looked surprised, 'Branching out huh Woody? My, you sure have things neat in here." He looked around on the shelves and floor. Everything seemed to be stacked in groups.

"Yeah I like to keep thing in order. I get teased about my room when friends come over. Everything is stacked in the order I took them."

"I believe it would be better to leave things in here as they are. I'll put a padlock on the door. Later we can transport them to the evidence room. I'll talk with your mom about it."

Woody's mother was very concerned about her son. "I'll do whatever you say Sheriff." She said as she twisted her hands. "I don't know what got into Woody. He has always been such a good boy."

"Yes ma'am, *Why do mothers always say that?"* he thought. "I would like to bring someone out tomorrow to see if some of the items belong to him. So if you see my car out here don't be alarmed."

"Well I guess that let's Woody off the hook for Leroy's murder. He was busy over in Greenville robbing the Odell's. Mr. Odell just identified his laptop." They were back at the station. Sheriff McCormick and Deputy Crane were going over the evidence again.

"We have ruled out Phillip Williams, the women from the church, Rev. Goodman, and now our neighborhood thief. There is no way possible that any of them could have done it. The only other person there was Lydia and she was unconscious. Anyway, she doesn't remember what happened. Lydia was the only other person there. Let's go over our notes and try to reconstruct the crime scene and go over the evidence again."

"Phillip Williams the insurance agent arrived first. He had an appointment with Leroy before he had to catch a flight to Chicago. The secretary said that Leroy insisted that Phillip meet with him about a policy. Why would he insist on this meeting? Make a note of it Douglas. We may need to follow up on that. When he got there he found the Martins. What did he find? You know we were so busy trying to find 'Who done it' we may be missing what others saw or heard. Maybe we need to contact Mr. Williams in Chicago. We know that he called 911 shortly after getting there. That matches the time it takes to drive out and the call that came in. Then according to The Reverend he was called and in turn he called the Church Committee. The paramedics found the house in disarray, people all over, Leroy on the floor dead and an unconscious Lydia. The coroner was called and he was performing his duties when we arrived. It took us awhile to get there because we were in Greenville talking with the sheriff of that county about breaking and entering because he thought it may be connected to our thief. We found he was correct."

"By the time we got there the entire area had been contaminated. The ladies had blood on them probably from Lydia. Lydia was on the sofa before the paramedics transported her to the hospital. According to them she had a bump and a cut on her head which was bleeding. Leroy was in a pool of blood. The tools behind him had blood on them. 'Any one of them could have been the weapon.' The tools on the floor were: a set of cotton scales, weights, a sledge hammer that went with the anvil behind Leroy's chair, a horse collar, and several plow heads. The wall behind him had been splattered with blood. On the wall was a crosscut saw, a bee smoker and some small farm items I didn't recognize. A lamp on a side table had blood on it. The preacher had stepped in the blood and a few footprints of his were on the floor. The blood had already coagulated before he stepped in it.

"The newest finger prints in the house were those of the people just mentioned. There is no indication that anyone else had been in the house for awhile. Since he was hit in the back of the head I don't see how it could be suicide. It seems that there were only two people in the house at the time of death, Leroy and Lydia. Leroy is dead. Lydia doesn't remember. I keep coming back to the same thing 'Lydia was the only other person there'."

"We're getting nowhere working on 'who', let's look at 'how'. Douglas we need to go talk with the coroner."

When they got there the coroner showed them pictures of the body and a transcript of the tape he made during the autopsy. "What killed him is this gash at the base of the skull. I made a plaster of Paris cast of the wound. There is a bump above that but it isn't severe enough to cause death. It could have happened when he hit the floor. Other than that there isn't anything else of significance. Most of the blood found in the house was that of Leroy's. Lydia's blood was confined to the sofa except for a small spot in the hall. We got Lydia's dress that she was wearing from the hospital. It had some of Leroy's blood on the bottom near the hem but it was smeared. After testing it I found that the blood had started to coagulate when it was smeared."

The sheriff rubbed his chin and thought out loud, "What was the weapon?"

He reached out to take the pictures, "Let's take a look at the pictures you made of the gash and the plaster cast of the indention. What in the room could have caused this? Since no one else was there the weapon must have been left in the room. I thought at first it was the weight but the weight would have made a bigger wound. The scales arm is not wide enough. What else could have been heavy enough? The sledge hammer, it sure is heavy enough? No, the head is too blunt it would make a big hole. The plow heads were still on the wall. They wouldn't cause too much damage anyway. What else? Douglas, you said that the blood on the brass lamp didn't look like splatters. You mentioned that it looked like someone had tried to wipe it off. Yes, the base of the lamp would be consistent with the wound. Now we're getting somewhere. It looks like we found our weapon."

"I just hate it that I keep coming back to 'Lydia was the only other person there'. I can't imagine Lydia as a murderer. She just isn't the type. Then again who is the type? If she did do it, how? Everything I come up with now is pure speculation."

"Time to hit the streets again we have a lot of footwork to do. We are going to go back to everyone we have already interviewed. We should start with people who were connected to each of the Martins. Here's the file on the people we have already talked with. Let's review that first. Then we can see if their account is the same as it was before."

Chapter 18

THE MARTIN'S NEAREST NEIGHBORS, BRUCE and Peggy Wilson live on the corner where the Martin drive begins. The older couple likes to sit on the front porch and watch the traffic. This country road is the main one going into Windfield. They said that there were very few visitors to the Martin farm. Leroy left out fairly early on Tuesday. Lydia could be seen driving a big farm truck out and return shortly with what appeared to be farm supplies. About once a week Lydia left around 8:30 AM in her old Chevy and returned around 11:30 that morning. Off and on Leroy went by in the truck. Nothing unusual happened until around about a few weeks before Leroy died. After supper they were sitting as usual on the porch when Lydia left out. She had not returned when they retired to bed. It was several days later Leroy left out while they were eating supper. They heard a loud roar and looked out to see his truck turn onto the main road. He nearly lost control as he fishtailed with his tires squealing. They went on to explain that they were not nosy people. Watching traffic was about all they could enjoy since they were not able to do anything else. But they would like to know what happened.

"Now that's interesting," remarked Sheriff McCormick as he slipped into the cruiser. "I wonder what happened, myself."

They didn't get much from Alice at the beauty shop, "Now Sheriff you know most of the talk in here is hearsay and gossip. And what's said in my shop stays in my shop. My customers know that I don't spread the gossip that I hear in here. I can't tell you anything about Leroy. But Lydia does a great job setting up my display window. She is very intelligent, efficient, works hard, and always on time, except for a few weeks ago. I may as well tell you this because my customers heard it. She came in late which was unusual for her. Leroy had detained her and she was quite upset with him because of it. Since it is not like Lydia to complain my customers noticed. Lydia apologized to them then completed the display. I thought she needed a night out so we met that evening at Denny's for coffee.

"So that's where she went when the Wilson's saw her leave. I think I'll just drop by Denny's for a cup of coffee."

"Why yes I remember Lydia coming in with Alice." Molly was more than willing to answer questions, "Her eyes were red like she had been crying. Alice was hovering over her like a mother hen. They stayed until I had to tell them that we were closing. That's not all several days later Leroy came in to eat supper. He has never done that before. I heard that he has, or had, a bad stomach and Lydia made a special effort to cook meals that wouldn't upset his digestive system. Boy he was in a snit that night. He nearly bit my head off. When we asked about it he told us to mind our own damn business."

The other merchants in town didn't add much to his notes. Lydia was well liked by them. Those she had worked for vouched for her business sense and her integrity. Leroy was well thought of as well. Sometimes he was a know-it-all but all in all he seemed to get along with everyone. He held several positions in the church and was known to lend a hand to help those in need.

Next on his list was Rev. Bradley Goodman, "Well Sheriff, what can I say? We lost a good Christian man when Leroy died. So, is it correct that you are calling it a homicide? I can't believe Leroy had an enemy in the world. He was one of the leaders of the church, a pillar of the community, would give you the shirt off his back."

"And what about Mrs. Martin isn't she a member of your church as well?"

"Well yes but she hasn't been attending since she caused a disturbance in church. I'm afraid she backslid. I think Leroy had his hands full after that. She may have had a nervous breakdown."

"How's that?" asked the sheriff, "What happened in church and what to makes you think she had a breakdown?"

"Well sheriff she stood right up in church and started telling us how to work on a stage. Can you believe it a woman brazen enough to stand up and speak out loud in church? We were all shocked of course. Leroy came to me for advice. He was worried about Lydia and as his pastor I helped him any way I could. Leroy said after that she started defying him and getting aggressive. She started going out at all hours of the night. She even refused to cook his supper one night. He had to go to town to eat. He told me about this and I gave him the name of a psychologist. Leroy had him visit one morning when Lydia was there. Of course he didn't tell Lydia he was a psychologist. He told Lydia that he was an old friend. The Doctor agreed that Lydia did have a nervous problem and needed help immediately."

"Wow! I'd hate to get on the wrong side of that man. I can't believe women aren't allowed to speak in his church." exclaimed Deputy Crane. "We really don't know what some people have to put up with until we start digging. I need something sweet to wash out my mouth or is it my ears. Who's next on the list?"

"I guess it's time to talk with the insurance agent who found the Martins. What was his name? Oh yes I remember, Phillip Williams. But he was leaving town when he found them. Since he was the one who found The Martins we should try to get in touch with him. Deputy, call the office here and find out all you can about Mr. Williams, where we can contact him and why he went to the Martin house."

Deputy Crane called the Windfield insurance branch office and asked about Mr. Williams and where could be located. L.C. Agnew, Phillip's replacement, said that he had been calling the Chicago headquarters trying to get in contact with Mr. Williams since he had just written an accident policy on the farm and needed to as how to handle it because of the circumstances. "Since there is some question as to whether it was an accident or murder I don't know how to handle a claim if it was filed. I don't know if I can tell you anything except that he upgraded Leroy's policy to cover new farm equipment. I haven't been able to contact Mr. Williams because he had a family emergency and left word with his secretary that he is not to be disturbed unless it was a dire emergency."

DANGEROUS OCCUPATION

"Lydia came by yesterday to see what needed to be done to file for a claim. Since she hasn't been back home, she didn't have the policy. She didn't even know where Leroy kept it. I found a copy of the policy and told her what necessary papers we needed to file. After I looked at it I noticed that it had a double indemnity for accidental death clause in it. And since you are now calling it a homicide I have been trying to contact Mr. Williams but he hasn't returned my calls. His secretary said that he has been very busy and also he has some type of emergency something about his sister."

Chapter 19

JULIE WILLIAMS WAS SINGING ALONG as drove the used motor home she had just bought. It was just large enough for her and her dog, Bear. They were headed for the open country to do some serious camping. She had made a few tentative plans but nothing definite.

"Touring the good old US is just what I need to get the burrs out of my hair." she sang making up the words as she drove along. After earning a degree in law and practicing with a large firm she could take no more of the corporate world. "I've had enough of stuffy clients, boring office parties and what suit to wear." She sang on. "If it don't rhyme what do I care. No one can hear me but you and me, Bear."

She let go with a hearty laugh. Bear was a tiny little mutt but his bark was large. She saw him in an alley as she walked to the law offices. He was a ball of shivering matted hair. Everyone laughed at her as she tried to wash him in the office kitchen sink.

"Get that rat out of here. We have important business to take care of here. What do you think you are doing anyway? Your apartment complex doesn't allow pets of any kind. And if you want to make partner, you'll get to your desk and finish those briefs that were due yesterday."

That's when Julie lost it and told her boss she had had enough of the big city. She felt like the little lost puppy, alone and cold in the jungle of buildings and strangers. After packing up her computer and the few items she kept at the office, Julie headed to the vet to have the little mutt checked out and to see if she had an ID chip. When she told the landlord that she had a little lost puppy she was sympathetic but explained that it was against rental policy and other tenants would not feel as sympathetic.

"I didn't see you carry the puppy up to your apartment, but tomorrow you will have to make other arrangements," she whispered.

That night while trying to find something on the TV to get her mind off her troubles, she turned to the travel channel where she saw an ad about a camper. The people were out in a park with children and pets.

"That's a sign," she thought, "I'll go camping. That's what I'll do. Three outrageous decisions in one day what in the world is wrong with me? Am I going crazy?"

Luck was on her side the next morning. She found a small motor home, bought it, stowed away her few possessions, and started out. The furnished rental apartment would be subleased to a young law student. Her landlord said she had been such a good tenant and kept everything clean and orderly that she had no problem renting it out. There were always law graduates looking for a place to stay.

"Well, Bear, it's you and me and the open road, for awhile anyway. I've saved enough to keep us alive for a few months. We don't need much do we, girl? We've been on the road for five hours and I'm getting hungry. What about a hamburger? While we eat I need to look in the campers guide for a campground. And before we get there I need to buy us some groceries. How does bacon and eggs in the morning sound? I do love that smell when we're camping. It reminds me of the time our family was in camping Alaska, Mom, Dad, Phillip and I. It was still light out at two in the morning. The only people out walking around were tourists. Locals knew when to sleep."

As Julie starred into the flame of the campfire that night she thought of her mother, Wilma. "I guess I had better bite the bullet and call her to let her know that her only daughter just quit her job." She pulled her cell phone out of her jeans pocket and saw that there was no signal.

Julie and Bear camped in the Ozarks of Missouri for a week before starting out again. While there they hiked trails, ate, slept, and read silly no-brainer books.

"Okay Bear, what do you think? Is it time to hit the trail again?" she closed her eyes and stabbed her finger on the US map. "Well, it looks like we will be headed west."

When she got on the main road, Julie called Wilma. "Hi Mom." Was all she got out before her mother yelled, "Julie, thank heavens you are alive. What happened? When you didn't answer your phone I called your office and was told that you walked out and no one knew where you went. I have been frantic. It has been a week. Where are you?"

"I know, Mom, I'm sorry. I tried to call but there was no signal where I was. Bear and I are having fun camping. I'll tell you all about it later. We are okay, Mom. Don't worry about us. I'm getting into heavy traffic, gotta go. By Mom."

"Bear? Who in the world is Bear? Oh Julie what has gotten into you? Dear God please take care of my precious daughter," she prayed.

When Wilma called Phillip's house to tell him that Julie had called he was still at work at the insurance headquarters. When he got in later that night his wife, Teresa, told him to call his mother. Their two children were already asleep.

Wilma explained why they had been unable to get in touch with Julie. "You know, Mom, that doesn't sound like Julie but I think she is missing Dad. They had such plans to practice together. Then he had to go and have that heart attack. I think she needs to sort things out. She has a good head on her shoulders, Mom. Dad worked long hours those last years. It took a toll out of him. She may be thinking along the same lines I am. Here I am working long hours and hardly seeing my family. My children are growing up and I'm not here long enough to enjoy them.

It was several weeks before Julie tired of the open road. "What do you think of visiting good old Phillip?" I bet he will really be surprised to see his vagabond little sister."

Phillip set aside a memo from the field office. It was something about a town of Windfield. He was so busy that he thought, "I'll look at it later. I just have to finish with this account. It really has so many snags I have to clean up. A million dollar deal is hanging on the insurance settlement."

"Mr. Williams, I hate to bother you since I know you are busy with the Southland Cooperation account but your mother is on line 3 and says it is an emergency."

"That's okay Sally put her on." A worried look came over Phillip's face. His mother did not call him at the office unless it was an emergency.

"Hi mom, what's up?"

"Oh Phillip," He could hear the tears in her voice. "Julie hit a semi in a little town in Iowa. She was transported to the hospital by medevac. I caught an emergency flight out. It leaves in 20 minutes. I'll call you when I hear how she is."

The emergency room was a mad house of noise when Wilma arrived by taxi. She rushed to the desk, "Julie Williams. I need to see Julie Williams. I am her mother."

The receptionist looked at the papers scattered on her desk. "There are several people who have just come in. Here it is Julie Williams, yes; she is in surgery at this time. If you have a seat in the waiting room I will get to you as soon as I can. I need to get some information about your daughter from you. By the way, Dr. Henski is the surgeon."

"Miss, please, I know you are busy but can you tell me anything about my daughter. How is she?

"Mrs. Williams, I know you are upset and worried about your daughter, but I don't know anything other than several people were transported here. It seems there were several cars involved. That's all I know I'm sorry. I'll let you know as soon as I hear."

Wilma walked into the waiting room in a daze. She was clutching her purse with both hands as she sat down. A couple approached her, "Mrs. Williams, we heard you say you were Julie's mother. We are Ira and Irma Helms. We were several cars behind the wreck and saw what happened. When we got there Julie was hurt but conscious. She asked us to take care of her little dog."

"Dog? What dog? Tell me how this happened?"

"The interstate was crowded but everyone seemed to be driving carefully because of the rain. The speed was fast but everyone was in their own lane. Then a motorcycle passed us. The driver was weaving around the other cars and trucks. When he swerved in front of the semi he slid on the wet pavement. Your daughter was behind the semi. When the driver of the big rig slammed on his breaks to avoid hitting the man, his rig jackknifed and your daughter's motor home plowed into the truck which was across two lanes. Julie was clutching this little bit of a dog. We live just a few miles north of here. So we came to check on your daughter. Her dog is fine, not a scratch on her. We left her at our house."

"Dog? Motor home? This is so confusing."

"Mrs. Williams?" Dr. Henski asked as he entered the waiting room an hour later. When Wilma looked up, he came over and sat on the edge of the sofa. "Your daughter is going to be alright. She has a broken leg, some internal injuries, and is quite bruised but I think she will be fine. You can see her when she gets out of recovery. She will be admitted and I want her to stay several days to heal and for observation. She will be sent to her room in a little while. I have to warn you that her face is quite bruised but that is from the airbag."

"Thank God," whispered Wilma. "Thank you Doctor."

When Dr. Henski turned to leave, Wilma asked about the others who were involved in the wreck. "It is amazing," He said, "All of them are alive, even the rider of the motorcycle. The troopers who worked the wreck told me that the driver of the semi did some fancy driving even though he jackknifed the truck he kept from hitting the cyclist. Your daughter did some fancy driving herself."

Chapter 20

"Looks like it's time to call out the big dogs for help," Sheriff McCormick said as he wiped his palm across his face. He was tired. After looking at his notes and trying to make sense of them he was at stand still.

All the notes and transcripts from the investigation tapes and notes from the coroner were laid out on several conference tables before the investigatory team including the district attorney. They divided up in groups. Each group was to examine all the evidence, discuss it among themselves, and come to a hypothesis or theory as to what happened. They spent all day sorting through the evidence and notes. When the groups reported back each came up with Lydia as the only person who could have done it. All the other people who were there had been ruled out as suspects. The neighborhood thief was no longer a suspect.

"Okay do we have enough to hold a probable cause hearing?" asked the district attorney. "What do we have so far? Lydia and Leroy were not getting along for some reason. Leroy thought Lydia was having a nervous breakdown. Lydia no longer went to church with Leroy even though we may think she had good reason for this. There are several reports of Lydia being very upset with Leroy and saying she couldn't take it anymore. Lydia had her bags packed and a plane ticket in her purse."

"I think we need to go back to work and come up with how she could have done it and why. We may have to work far into the night. I want the evidence to still be fresh in our minds. This time let's try brainstorming. It seems that the weapon was the brass lamp, which had been wiped off. As I go over each piece of evidence fell free to add your thoughts. We have to come up with a plausible explanation. I realize that all the evidence will be circumstantial but that's all we have for now."

Several offered an explanation. "Let's say they had a fight. There is evidence that something was going on with them. The fight got out of hand. Lydia picked up the lamp and cracked it over his head. But there isn't any sign of a struggle and Leroy was hit in the back of the head. Why would he turn his back if they were fighting?"

"You're right about there not being evidence of a struggle. But the other scenario that she hit him when his back was turned may work."

'One of the church committee ladies," the sheriff searched his notes. "Ah yes, here it is, Amy, said that the rocker was turned over on Leroy and she and Rev. Goodman set the rocker back up because she knew that Lydia was a neat housekeeper. So it seems that Leroy may have been sitting in the rocker when he was hit."

"If Lydia hit Leroy then how did she get knocked out?" The evidence clearly shows that she was unconscious and was so for two weeks."

"There were all kinds of metal tools on the floor maybe one of them fell and hit her. Maybe it was an accident."

"Somebody slipped up behind Leroy, hit him in the back of his head with a brass lamp and it was an accident?"

"If it was an accident why were her bags packed and why did she have a flight ticket in her purse?"

"If she was so upset with Leroy, why didn't she just leave him? She had a plane ticket."

"Well maybe it was for insurance. How much was Leroy worth?"

"Hey that's something we need to look into. I remember the reason for Mr. Williams being there. He is an insurance salesman." The sheriff shifted through his notes again. "I thought there was something nagging at me. The policy that Leroy just recently took out had a double indemnity clause in it for accidental death."

"Now we're getting somewhere."

"But Lydia has always been such an honest person. She was always involved in helping the community. Her Aunt Ruth set up the Shiphrah

House for those in need of a safe harbor and Lydia worked there when she could."

"But I have heard that she hasn't been working there as much as she used to."

"There were some people that we talked with commented that Lydia had lost some of her spark. She even seemed to be sad or depressed. She didn't come to town as often and when she did she was always in a hurry. The building contractor said that she wasn't taking as many work assignments as before. "

"Maybe the preacher was right. He said that Leroy thought she was having a nervous breakdown."

"Lydia's account of what happened is always the same, just not the exact words. So it isn't like she made up a story and memorized a script. I hate to think Lydia could do such a thing, she has always been such a nice friendly well liked person."

"We have gone over and over the evidence. I don't see anything else we can do but hold a probable cause hearing."

"You just don't know how I hate this job at a time like this. There is nothing I hate worse than bringing in a suspect that has always been a model citizen, an asset to the community."

Chapter 21

Kate called Lydia on her cell phone, "Dee where are you? I called your home phone and it is still full. I called your cell phone and it went straight to the mailbox. Are you alright?"

"Oh Kay, it has been such a turmoil here. Everything seems to be happening. I haven't been home since I was in the hospital. That's the reason the answering machine is full. The sheriff keeps telling me that the house is a crime scene and I can't go back home until they finish. Kay I need you when are you coming?"

"That's what I'm calling about. I'm on my way to the airport now. Can you pick me up when I land? We'll talk when I get there."

"Of course I'll pick you up. Oh, Kay I can't wait to see you."

When Kate walked out in the airport, the two friends rushed into each other's arms and held on for awhile. "Dee, it is so good to see you. I've been so worried," *and you have lost so much weight,* she thought.

Lydia had booked an efficiency suite for them at the hotel where she was now staying. She had moved from the bed and breakfast for privacy reasons and she no longer needed the personal help. They stayed up all night catching up on things.

The conversation kept switching back and forth from what has been going on since they had visited each other to the present situation.

"I have been so worried about you because you just haven't sounded like yourself lately. I could hear it over the phone. That's the reason I insisted that you come. The ticket I sent you was a bribe that I hoped you would take."

Lydia had kept so much bottled up it seemed that Kate broke the dam and everything came gushing out.

"I hate to say this since Leroy is dead but you are right Kate, things have not been good between Leroy and me for some time. It seems everything I suggested was stupid. I wanted to make gardening easier because I just couldn't keep up with the weeds. When I told him I read in a gardening magazine about making rows closer together to cut down on the area that needed hoeing, he said that I knew nothing about farming. I didn't tell him that Aunt Ruth and I always had a garden. So I knew a little about it. I just kept my mouth shut to keep from having an argument. When I suggested that I get a garden tiller you'd think I wanted a bulldozer. He said that I couldn't handle a tiller. Again I kept my mouth shut. I didn't remind him that he sent me to the feed and seed store in the big dual wheel truck to pick up supplies."

"Then he made me mad when he had a friend over and kept insisting that I stay and visit when he knew I had a window display to finish. I finally told him that I had to go. He didn't like it but I didn't give him time to tell me so. I was so angry that he made me late I nearly lost it at Alice's beauty shop. When I told Alice why I was late I was so frustrated the ladies in the shop even stopped their gossip to listen in. I did apologize to them and went to work on the window. I was so embarrassed."

Kate laughed, "Well you made their day. I bet that was material for at least a week"

"But we really had it out when HE decided that I was not going to visit you until September. I didn't keep my mouth shut that time I told him I WAS going. That's when he really lost it. He yanked your picture from the wall and threw it on the floor. It shattered to pieces."

"Oh, I'm so sorry about the trouble that my invitation caused you. But I knew something was wrong. Now you have all this to contend with. Dee you know I would have been here had I known you were in the hospital. And poor Leroy was buried without you there. I can't imagine the preacher taking over like that. You really have had a terrible time. Now you tell me that the sheriff thinks it was a homicide. Who do they think did it?"

"That's just it; Kay, as far as I know they don't have a suspect yet and I can't come up with anyone who would do such a thing. I know Leroy was a braggart and know-it-all which grated on some people's nerves but that's not enough to make someone kill him. I just don't remember what happened after I went to the bathroom except a loud noise like something big fell. Leroy kept heavy farm tools on the wall behind what I call 'Leroy's corner' and a set of cotton scales is always falling. Maybe that's what I heard. Then I think something hit me in the head. The next thing I remember is I woke up in the hospital with a terrific headache and a gash on my head."

"They say I was in a coma for two weeks. While I was out Leroy was buried, my house and farm have been off limits, and the sheriff and his crew have been all over my house rummaging through everything. There's no telling how the house looks by now. I haven't been allowed to go see or clean it.

"At first the sheriff was very concerned about my health and seemed to be working hard to sort out what happened. He even arranged for me to stay in a bed and breakfast because he did not want me to go back to the house 'just yet'. He said that I would be better off there where I could have my meals supplied and medical attention would be close. It would be good also because there would be someone to help since I still a little wobbly on my feet. I did have two friends who offered to take turns with me at home but I was not allowed to go there."

"Wait a minute, maybe he wasn't being nice after all, maybe that is his way of dealing with people to get their confidence. Now that I look back I remember that he said I was not to go anywhere. Every time when he came to ask me if I remembered anything else about what happened, he reminded me to stay in the county. Now why would he do that? He said that he needed me to be available if he had other questions. Now I wonder if that's the real reason. The last time we talked he did grate on my nerves and made me a little angry about the plane ticket you sent and my packed bags. Now that my brain is beginning to function better, I wonder if I was a little naïve and too trusting. But you know me Kay. I'm a trusting person. I trust people until they give me a reason not to. Sometimes that has caused me a problem especially in the business world."

'Oh I forgot another thing." Lydia laughed "I was almost excommunicated from Beulah Land Community Church."

"You what?"

"Oh yeah, I dared to stand right up and speak right out loud in church. I truly didn't know that women weren't allowed to speak in that church. I stood up right there and explained that a stage was in danger of splitting apart if they substituted a part that didn't fit. When I heard the universal gasp I thought it was because I, a female, was dealing in technology that was a male realm. I was escorted out by Leroy as the good reverend demanded. It wasn't funny then, but it is now that I look back on it. You should have seen the look on their faces as if they couldn't believe that God didn't strike me dead right then and there. Even though I sent an apology to the congregation with Leroy I never set foot in that church again. I did feel bad about upsetting some but not the entire congregation that's why I sent the apology which the preacher demanded and Leroy wanted. Of course I played around with wording so that I just said that I was sorry for upsetting the congregation."

"Oh yes, I might add, I heard via the grapevine, Alice's shop, that my advice was ignored and indeed the stage was rendered asunder. You should have heard the women in the shop laughing and all talking at the same time about men running in all directions dodging flying debris. Of course Leroy never mentioned it."

They were rolling with laughter when the telephone rang.

When the telephone rang in the suite Lydia answered. She put her hand over the mouthpiece and mouthed, "It's Sheriff McCormick". "Yes Sheriff, what can I do for you today?" she answered with a sugary sweet voice. "You need to talk with me again? Well why don't you just sit tight in the lobby and I'll be right down? The lobby won't do? You need to come up here?" She held the telephone to one side so that Kate could hear as well. "By all means come on up."

Lydia opened the door to the sheriff and a female deputy. Lydia and Kate stood in the doorway wondering --- "What in the world?"

"Lydia we need to come in out of the hallway, the sheriff had a stern look on his face the deputy's face had a somber expression.

Lydia and Kate stepped aside and let them enter as she introduced Kate.

"I didn't want to do this in public. It is already as unpleasant as it gets. You just don't know how I hate to do this. But Lydia, I am going to have to take you in and book you."

Both Kate and Lydia were in shock. They stood there with mouths open as the sheriff spouted the 'You have the right'… spiel.

"WHAT?" yelled Kate as she grabbed for Lydia. "Hasn't she been through enough already? Her husband has been killed and now you arrest her?"

"Well well what happened to the sympathetic lawman who is just asking questions so he can find the truth? I can think of two clichés that fit. Could it be that I 'invited the fox into the henhouse'? Or is it 'a wolf in sheep's clothing'?" Lydia questioned with a scowl on her face.

"Now Lydia let's not make it any harder than it is. If you come quietly without a fuss, I won't have to put handcuffs on you and we can walk out without anyone knowing what's going on."

"Yeah right, I am escorted out by the sheriff and a deputy and everyone thinks we are going for a stroll in the park. Town gossip will beat us to the courthouse."

"I can see it now. Tongues wagging, speculation flying and Alice will have customers lined up who all of a sudden have an emergency and need their hair done."

"What are you going to do with Lydia, Sheriff?"

"I am going to carry her in and book her. The district attorney will set the date for a preliminary hearing to show probable cause since what we have is circumstantial."

"Can I come with her?"

"I'm afraid not but I will allow you to come down but you can't be with her while I book her. You might want to take her personal items with you since she can't have them in jail."

"Jail she's going to jail?"

"I'm afraid so since the charge is murder."

"Murder? This gets worse by the second."

"Can't you hear them Kay? 'Can you believe mousy little Lydia's a murderer?' The press will have a field day. They will try me, find me guilty, executed, and buried by this time tomorrow. Ain't life just wonderful?"

Chapter 22

Lydia called her attorney Felix Fields right after she was arrested. Even though he had been Leroy's attorney she did not know him. She did not feel that he helped her at all when she was questioned at the hospital. But she did not know anyone else to call. When she talked with him she told him the same thing that she had told the sheriff over and over.

"Mr. Fields I have no idea why they arrested me. This is ridiculous. You were there when I talked with the sheriff. So you have heard what I know. I don't know what happened to Leroy. I didn't see anything because I was coming from the bathroom which is located in the back near our bedroom. I heard a noise which may have been one of the tools falling. It probably was the cotton scales which would not stay on the wall. Then I was hit in the head."

"Did you see anyone there who could have hit you?"

"No. I guess I could lie and tell you that I saw someone. Maybe that would get me off the hook. But I didn't. I was hit in the forehead. So if anyone was there I probably would have seen him. When I woke up I was in the hospital."

Lydia, I have to ask you this. Did you kill your husband? Maybe it was an accident. Maybe you didn't mean to."

"No! I did not kill Leroy."

"How can you be so sure? You say you don't remember some things. Maybe certain sections of your memory are missing."

'I don't think I have a lapse of memory. I was just unconscious."

"Okay. Then tell me anything else you CAN remember. How did the house look after you were hit?"

By this time Lydia was getting a little perturbed with Felix Fields.

"I can't tell you how the house looked after that. I was **unconscious.** Later I wasn't there. I was in the hospital. The only people who can answer that are the people who were there. And I don't even know for sure who they were because I wasn't there. I have to take the sheriff's word for it. **I was not there!**"

"Now, Lydia getting huffy with me isn't helping."

"Okay. What do I do now? Since I haven't been **arrested** before, I don't know the order of things. Maybe I need to talk with a criminal. He would probably give me some good pointers and tell me what to expect."

"Lydia there is no need to get sarcastic."

"Well what do you expect? My husband has been killed. I have been in the hospital in a coma. My husband was buried without my authority. I haven't been allowed to go home. Now I find myself arrested and hauled off in front of my best friend. There's no telling who else was in the hotel when I was so unceremoniously escorted out. How do you **think** that makes me feel?"

"Okay. If you calm down I'll try to explain what usually happens in a case like this. This is the usual way these proceedings go. You will appear before a magistrate. This should be within forty-eight hours of your arrest. The magistrate will advise you of the charges. Based on information supplied by the district attorney he will decide if there is probable cause to hold you. At this appearing you, the suspect, will not be given the opportunity to introduce evidence. If the magistrate finds there isn't enough evidence to hold you may leave. But if the district attorney finds more evidence later on you could be charged again. If he finds there is sufficient evidence to detain you there are several options he may choose. He could set bail but in cases such as murder the suspect is usually held in detention until a preliminary hearing is held. This could take up to ten days if you are detained or up to twenty days if you are not. Now, does that answer your question?"

DANGEROUS OCCUPATION

"Well, I guess so but it sure didn't make me feel better. As a matter fact I am scared to death."

"Sheriff, this is the most outrageous thing I have ever heard," Kate was in the sheriff's office. "How could anyone possibly think that Lydia could do such a thing? She in one of the most revered people I know. She has always given so much to this community. I want to know what evidence you have that proves that Lydia is a murderer. Did someone see her do it?"

"Now Kate, you know I can't give you that information or reveal our sources. Lydia has representation and it would be best if you stay out of it."

"What do you mean stay out of it? I'm already **in it** because Lydia is my best friend and I want to know what is going to happen to her."

"She is going to be brought before a magistrate in a couple of days to see if there is probable cause to hold her for murder. If there isn't then she will be free to go at least for the time being.'

"What do you mean 'for the time being'?"

"She could be recharged. Okay. I have told you all I am allowed to. Now I **do** have other duties to take care of. So if you don't mind would you please go away so I can get to them?"

The magistrate read the charge of premeditated murder and asked if Lydia had counsel. Attorney Fields identified himself. After hearing from the district attorney the magistrate leaned forward, "Mrs. Martin even though the evidence is mostly circumstantial I find that there is enough to hold a preliminary hearing where you will be allowed to present evidence to the contrary. Since this is a murder case you will remain in custody. This hearing will take place a week from today. Will that give you enough time to prepare?" He looked questioningly at both attorneys.

Both the district attorney and Mr. Fields said yes.

Before Lydia was returned to jail Felix spoke to her, "I'll see you tomorrow and we will go over our strategy. In the meantime I want you to think of anything that might help your defense".

That afternoon Kate was allowed a few minutes to visit Lydia in jail, "Kay what am I going to do? They say that I am the only one who could have killed Leroy. There are witnesses to testify that Leroy and I weren't getting along. Someone overheard me say that I couldn't take it any longer."

It was late in the afternoon the next day when Mr. Fields showed up at the jail to talk with Lydia, "I have been talking with the district attorney. He gave me some of the information he had but not much. At the hearing he will present the facts found by the sheriff's investigation and accounts of the witnesses. Most likely he will present just enough to show probable cause."

"But what evidence could he have that I did it? What proof does he have? I can't possibly come up with an answer."

"But he would not have gone this far if he did not believe he had enough to go to trial and prove his point. And if it gets that far we need strong argument to prove you didn't do it."

"But what about 'innocent until proven guilty'?"

"Well that's so but there have been times when a person is found guilty on circumstantial evidence when there was no other reasonable answer. At this hearing hearsay can be used. And there seems to be a lot of that. Now don't get me wrong there aren't a lot of people out there who want to see you behind bars. As a matter of fact they don't want that. But when they were asked about your actions lately there seems to be a problem. Some of the hearsay is that you and Leroy were at odds with each other. You were very upset when he made you late for a job at the beauty shop. And later at Denny's diner you were seen in an agitated state. Then Leroy seemed to be very angry at you. All this happened just before the uh, uh, accident. Your prints of course were inside the house along with the others who came in later. Your neighbors who live at the end of your driveway saw no one else come in that day until Mr. Williams came by. Since watching traffic seems to be their only source of entertainment, their testimony is crucial."

"Just whose side are you on anyway? Of course my prints are all over the house. I lived there you know. And yes I was a little upset with Leroy. Married couples do have spats off and on you know. And so what about the Wilsons not seeing anyone come in? If I were going to kill somebody I certainly would not come in that way. I'd sneak in the back."

"Are you sure that there isn't anything else you can remember about that day something I can use in your defense?"

"Again, no I don't. The last thing I remember when I was at home was something hitting my head. I didn't see anyone there. I didn't see Leroy after I came back from the bathroom because I was just coming around the corner."

"Then we have very little to go on in your defense except your word and character witnesses. I guess we will just have to wait and see what the district attorney has and work from there.

The preliminary hearing was held a week later in the courtroom. There were only a few witnesses in the courtroom. The Reverend Bradley Goodman was one and as usual a reporter from the press was there. The judge looked down from his lofty seat and advised Lydia of her rights and then read the charge of premeditated murder.

The district attorney presented the evidence to the judge. The factual reports from the sheriff's and the coroner's investigations showed Leroy's blood on the brass lamp. The lamp had been wiped off so that there were no finger prints on it. There was Leroy's blood on Lydia's dress.

Then circumstantial evidence was from reports taken from members of the community. Lydia's behavioral change was cited.

It seemed that Lydia's personality had changed. She no longer worked with the needy as she had before. She no longer attended the community church. She was always in a hurry and didn't visit with friends when she came to town. She stopped taking on assignments for window displays. She didn't work as the interior designer for the building contractor.

Lydia and Leroy had been at odds with each other. The scene at Alice's beauty shop was brought out. She was very angry at Leroy and was heard to say that she couldn't take it anymore. She was clearly angry at Leroy for making her late. She was seen later that evening at Denny's Diner in an agitated state. The statement form Molly was read. Lydia had obviously been crying when she met Alice at the diner. It was brought out that Lydia and Alice stayed at the diner until it closed. This was not typical of either woman but especially of Lydia. Then, the statement continued on, later that week Leroy came in for supper which too was not typical because Leroy usually ate supper at home. Leroy was very angry.

Then the Reverend Goodman was called to the stand. He did not paint a very pretty picture of Lydia. The first incident that he brought out was the Christmas window display where Lydia had a cat with his tail being caught by the rocker. The preacher considered it a sadistic tendency. He cited several conversations that he had with Leroy where Leroy thought Lydia was not respectful to him as a wife should be to her husband. He thought that Lydia was trying to take over his role as head of the household. Then he told the judge that she caused a disturbance in the church and upset the entire congregation with her sinful ways. "Leroy was worried about Lydia's behavior and wondered if she was having a nervous breakdown. That's when I suggested that he call a psychologist to evaluate her. I gave him the name of one. Leroy had him come to the house without Lydia knowing who he was."

"What?" Lydia gasped out loud and looked at the preacher and then her lawyer. "I don't know anything about seeing a psychologist." She was quite upset that her lawyer had not spoken once to object to any of the testimony given so far. She leaned over to ask him why he had not said a word in her defense. Felix turned to her with anger in his eyes, "You never told me about seeing a psychologist. I asked you if there was anything else that I should know and you never mentioned this. I can't help you if you don't tell me the truth."

Now Lydia was furious "I didn't know that Leroy was so devious as to have a psychologist talk with me while pretending it was a friend."

The judge looked at Felix, "Counselor is there something you wish to say."

"No, your honor." Replied Mr. Fields

"The judge frowned at Felix then directed his words to the preacher, "Is there anything else you have to say?"

"Yes, the psychologist did indeed feel that Lydia was having a nervous breakdown because the entire time he was there she continued to twist her hands and seemed to be in a tizzy."

At this the judge coughed and asked, "Does the counselor wish to question the witness?"

"No questions your honor sir," Felix half rose and sat back down.

The next evidence was the plane ticket and the packed bags "It is obvious that Lydia had plans to leave shortly before Leroy was killed. Blood on the alleged weapon had been wiped off. Why would the lamp be wiped off if not to destroy finger prints? Then we found a broken picture frame in the trash. This is evidence that there had been some type of altercation."

"You went through my trash?" Lydia rose and spoke to the attorney before she thought. Felix took her arm and pulled her back down into her chair. Lydia jerked away. She did not like what was going on. She felt like a sheep being led to slaughter.

"Mrs. Martin do you have something to say?" asked the judge.

"No your honor," answered Felix before she could answer. Then he turned to Lydia, "It is in your best interest that you say nothing at this time," he whispered. "If you do then the prosecuting attorney will be given the opportunity to question you."

"But I have nothing to hide." Lydia was getting to the end of her rope with Felix.

"Trust me on this I'm the attorney here. You do not want to say a word at this time."

Then another bombshell fell, "The prosecution asks that no bail because of the flight risk. As it has already been brought out Lydia had bags packed and a plane ticket ready to flee."

Again Felix Fields said nothing.

"Even though the evidence Linking Lydia to the homicide is circumstantial, Lydia will be brought to trial and she is to remain in jail until such time." The judge rapped the gavel and left the bench.

The next day Kate visited Lydia in jail. She was allowed to visit with supervision. After giving Lydia a big hug she brought good wishes from several friends that knew she was going to visit. "Some of the testimonies brought by the district attorney were from friends that were just trying to help in solving the case. Your friends wanted me to let you know that they didn't know that what they told the sheriff would be held as evidence against you. They wanted me to let you know that they are so sorry. They had no idea that what they told the sheriff would be held against you. They said that they were just talking." Kate was given only a few minutes to visit. She promised to return the next day if she was allowed to visit.

After Kate left Felix paid a visit, "I don't know what else you are holding back from me."

Exasperated Lydia Yelled "I am not holding back anything. I haven't seen a psychologist. I don't know what he is talking about."

"And you don't remember what happened when Leroy was killed."

"No! I don't know what happened."

"You don't remember seeing a psychologist and you say that you don't remember what happened. You had your plane ticket and your bags packed. You don't deny any of this. Then you could be suffering from partial amnesia. I think your best bet is to try for a plea bargain."

"Plea bargain? Are you out of your ever-loving mind? What kind of lawyer are you anyway? You never once questioned any of the evidence brought against me. I don't know what ever possessed me to hire you."

"Hey I'm the only lawyer you got." He picked up his briefcase.

"I wonder what he has in that briefcase. He has not once opened in front of me."

Felix turned and looked down his nose at Lydia as he prepared to leave, "Let me know what you decide. I am giving the best advice I know under the circumstances. Oh and by the way your friend, Kate is that it? You might want to know that she could be charged with accessory before the fact." At that the door to her cell closed behind him.

Chapter 23

Lydia paced her cell and prayed all night after Felix told her that Kate may be arrested as an accomplice. She was afraid that Kate would be arrested when she returned for a visit as she had promised. She spent the night praying that God would give her guidance, patience, and an answer. She also asked God what was happening and why. Without sleep and sick with worry she was disheveled and wild-eyed by the time Kate came.

Lydia had been up all night trying to think what to do. When Kate came in to visit she could hardly speak clearly. She had so much to say her words were tripping over themselves. Everything she had thought of saying during the night was coming out all at once. "Kay listen to me you have to leave now!" whispered Lydia as she looked around to see if anyone heard her.

"Kate was so shocked at Lydia's appearance she started to cry, "Oh Dee, What have they done to you? You're not making any sense." She was beginning to think that they were right about Lydia having a nervous breakdown.

When Lydia insisted that she go home immediately Kate thought she meant back at the hotel. She couldn't think of a thing back there that was that important. "What's wrong Dee? What else has happened? Do you need for me to go get something? I can go right now and get it."

"No, no Kay you must leave here. It's not me I'm worried about. It's you Kay. I want you to hurry, go, leave Windfield, now!"

"I am not going anywhere until you tell me what's going on." She crossed her arms across her chest and looked Lydia in the eye. "Now you calm down and talk."

"Okay, okay but you have to listen carefully. I am not crazy. I know I sound crazy but I am not. I know I must be talking in circles. Because I have been up all night thinking and worrying what I'm saying is just coming out wrong. It's like you stepped right into the middle of the conversation. So I'll try to explain quickly and clearly. Felix told me that you could be charged with helping me because I was going to visit you. He said that you could be arrested as an accomplice. I want you to leave now, Kay. I need for you to leave before something happens to you. You must get away fast before you are arrested for helping me.

"Dee this is crazy. But you are making more sense than when I came in. Are you sure I could be arrested? What **if** Mr. Fields says that I could be arrested? He didn't impress me when I met him."

"Felix wants me to make a plea bargain. He wants to argue that I have PARTIAL amnesia. He must think I'm guilty and you helped me plan it."

Kate put her hands on her hips and frowned, "I don't know how much you can believe what he says as truth. He doesn't seem to be too bright anyway with him wanting you to plead guilty. I just can't believe I could be arrested."

"Well, would you have believed that I would be charged with murder? Here I am sitting in jail. It happened. Go home back to Minnesota, Kay. You can help me there. I need for you to get me another lawyer. You can't help me if you too are in jail

"You're right. You are here. Now you have me convinced. Don't worry, I'm on my way. Samuel and I will get you a real lawyer. Now you just sit tight right here don't go anywhere until I get back". A corner of Lydia's mouth lifted at Kate's joke attempt.

On the way back to the hotel Kate called Samuel who helped to get her a seat on the next flight out of Windfield. He was shocked to learn all that had happened to Lydia. Kate had been talking with him every day but now he could see how things had gone down fast. He was surprised that things had progress this far. He had been telling Kate not to worry so much that all would work out. Now he wasn't so sure. It seemed that things were totally out of hand. It was ridiculous to think Lydia capable of murder. After he got off the phone talking with Kate he called a friend who recommended Jim Osborn a lawyer he knew.

Samuel met the exhausted Kate at the airport. She grabbed her two children and squeezed them both. Jamie scrambled out of his mother's grasp. "Mom not so hard," cried Ruthie, "You act as if you've been gone a year not two weeks." Kate welcomed the hug and kiss that Samuel gave her. "It seems like a year to me." He said as he took the carry-on bag she had on her shoulder and wrapped his arm around her waist. "Let's head for baggage claim and get your mother home." "No baggage Sam. I left everything else back in Windfield. Lydia made me promise that I would leave quickly. She was so worried that I would be arrested." When she said 'arrested' Ruthie gasped, "Mom!"

"Now don't you worry about your mom. She is going to be fine and so is your Aunt Dee. I have a colleague working on it right now. As soon as he clears up a case he is working on he's going to pounce right on it like a wildcat. That prosecuting attorney in Windfield will think a tornado hit town." He had them all laughing as they headed home.

Sheriff McCormick assigned Lydia to the minimum security unit while awaiting trial because his staff was shorthanded with his most competent officer, Russ Carter, in the hospital. Since there were video cameras everywhere he was confident that she would not be able to escape from his facility. He also made sure that her cell was well away from the more violent inmates. *"I know she must hate me by now but I was just doing my job. I wish that her lawyer would do his. She doesn't know it but I'm still trying to make sense of this whole mess. If she did kill Leroy she must have been temporally insane from all she had endured."* The sheriff shook his head sadly and picked up a folder and started working on another case.

Some of the women moaned when Mrs. Lattimer walked in Alice's shop. She was a sweet lady but very hard of hearing and talked loudly because of it. Alice's mind was on Lydia as she trimmed a customer's hair. The gossip was still about Lydia being charged with murder. But it had settled down to a daily curiosity about what was going on at that time. Most of those who frequented the beauty shop were sympathetic toward Lydia. Alice was so worried she had trouble keeping her thoughts on anything else. Then her attention was brought back sharply when Mrs. Lattimer came in. She couldn't help but overhear Mrs. Lattimer who was talking over the noise in the shop. She was talking so loudly other customers were complaining about it. Alice was afraid that she would have to ask her to lower her voice but didn't have to because another customer broke in, "Mrs. Lattimer did I hear you say that you had a sister who lives in Chester? I have a grand niece who lives there. Isn't that such beautiful historic town?" The noise level returned to the normal buzz as the two women continued in conversation. *"Thank you Lord for giving me the patience to hold my tongue,"* whispered Alice.

As she was leaving Mrs. Lattimer told her new friend goodbye. "You tell your brother-in-law that I hope he gets out of the hospital soon. I will put him on my prayer list. I do hope he finds someone who knows how to cook his meals when he gets out of the hospital. That job he has at our county jail could be what's causing his stomach problems. The stress there is enough to make anybody sick"

Molly was shopping in the local dress shop when she bumped into Alice. "My goodness Alice I nearly knocked you down. Are you alright?" Alice looked up with a dazed look on her face, "I'm fine Molly. I just wasn't watching where I was going. I am so worried about Lydia."

"I was just about to ask how she was. I haven't been able to visit her yet."

"You know Lydia she has always been a busy person and just sitting in that jail is not good for her. She's lost so much weight in the few days she has been there. Visitors can't stay very long and there's nothing to do but walk the floor and think. Molly it's so sad. I hate to see her waste away like this. I wish there was something we could do."

As they were talking Sophia walked up, "I know you are talking about Lydia. I went to see her today. It's not good girls. We have to do something.

Let's get out of here. I tell you what, let's go to my office and put our heads together." I'll call Matty to meet us there. Surely we can find something to help."

They walked into a large bright realtor's office on the corner. The light came in from widows which stretched across the entire side wall. A large cherry desk and comfortable office chair was in a corner. Book shelves filled with pamphlets and brochures were behind the desk. On the other side wall a plush green sofa faced the windows. In the middle of the room was a round table with chairs. It was a room inviting you to come in and browse. They went up to the second floor where there several offices, a conference room, and a kitchen with small modern appliances. Sophie made tea in the kitchen while the others set out goodies they had bought on the way.

They sat with long sad faces in a conference room as they drank tea and talked about what to do for Lydia. "We don't even know how long she will have to stay waiting for her trial to come up. It's terrible. I can't believe the judge agreed to deny bail. The way I feel right now I wish this stuff was a little stronger," Molly sighed as she lifted her tea cup.

"This is depressing. Sitting around with long faces isn't helping Lydia at all," Matty said as she stood up and picked up her purse. "We are in such a sorry state I don't think we'll get anywhere tonight. Why don't we go home and get refreshed? Maybe our brains can work better tomorrow."

"Okay, let's meet at Matty's first thing tomorrow and compare notes." Sophie called as they were leaving. "No on second thought tomorrow is Tuesday. You know that's when the Beulah Land Church has breakfast. Let's meet back here at my office after work."

"Sophia walked into Matty's the next morning for breakfast just ahead of Alice. As they passed the pastor's table they acknowledge his presence with a broad fake grin and nod. "Good morning ladies. This is getting to be a pleasant habit with you two." Matty greeted them with a smile. "Good Morning, Matty," they said in unison as they took a seat in a booth. Matty brought their orders out and sat down with them since she had only a few customers. As they enjoyed the meal Alice couldn't help but remember the conversation she overheard back at her shop. "I just can't get this out of my head. It keeps nagging at me for some reason. Anyway, there was a lady in my shop whose brother-in-law works as overseer of the jail. Maybe it's because I know poor Lydia is there where he works. It seems he has the same digestive problem that Leroy had. I remember Lydia telling me how she had to be very careful about preparing his meals. I don't know why it bothers me. I don't even know the man."

"I know what you mean about Leroy having to watch his diet. Every Tuesday he would come in and eat "the usual" which for Leroy was a slice of country ham, two eggs, biscuit, gravy and coffee. Lydia told me that then every Tuesday after the church breakfast he would come home complaining about his stomach. Even if he had digestive problems, I wasn't about to tell Leroy that he shouldn't eat his usual. Not in front of his pals. He would have fit. I can see his red face now with steam blowing out his ears," Laughed Matty as she blew out her cheeks and raised her arms in the air.

"Matty," called the Reverend Goodman, I need a refill of coffee here if you're **not too busy**."

"I know he is just dying to know what we are up to," Matty pointed her head toward him." The old sourpuss hasn't gotten over the time I asked him to leave when he was calling Lydia a sinner. But he still comes here because I serve the best breakfast in town," she whispered out of the side of her mouth as she rose from the booth. She picked up the pot and went over and plastered a smiled on her face as she poured his coffee. "Can I get you anything else, Sweetie?"

"Humph," was the answer.

The group was back at Sophie's Office, "Does anyone have an idea about what we can do for Lydia?" Sophie asked.

"Maybe we could carry her one of your special cakes, Matty," Offered Alice.

"I don't think so. Lydia is a much better cook than all of us put together. I'm not throwing off on our cooking but you know what I say is true. Remember that cooking contest we had a few years ago? Lydia won blue ribbons on every dish she entered.

"I wish I had a piece of her strawberry pie right now, mmm," Molly rolled her eyes as she remembered the taste."

"Food, food, food, is there nothing we can do except talk about food. This is getting us nowhere." Sophie slammed her fist down on the table so hard they all jumped. "I'm so sorry. It just makes me so angry that they locked up Lydia like a common criminal." "I know," said Alice. "She can't even get out on bail. The justice system stinks."

"**Food**, that's it!" yelled Sophie. They all looked at her with open mouths. Didn't she just slam her fist on the table because we were discussing food?

"Alice, what was that woman's name who has a brother-in-law with digestive problems? Didn't you say that he works in the jail where Lydia is housed?"

"Well yes, Mrs. Carter was her name," Alice's eyes grew large as the idea hit. "She was so worried about him when he was hospitalized because of stomach problems. That may be something to work on. I need to get back to the shop to look up her number." Alice grabbed her purse and left.

"Asa," Molly pointed up in the air as if a light came on. The ideas were beginning to take hold. "Asa knows someone who works at the jail. "I need to go talk with my bossy boss."

Chapter 24

"Thank you for finding me something to do. You are a life saver. Looks like God did answer my prayer even though it is not all I prayed for. I guess maybe I have to be more patient but Lord it is hard. I was going stir crazy in that cell. I want you to tell Asa that I'm glad he knows people in high places especially the chief correctional officer here," Lydia grinned knowing that Asa would laugh at that. "Mr. Carter has been so good to me since I started preparing his meals." She told her friends. "I'm sure that's why he let all four of you to visit at the same time. I guess he wants me to continue cooking for him." She smiled the color already coming back in her face.

Alice was so happy to see Lydia in better spirits. "Mrs. Carter, his sister-in-law stops by my shop even when she has no appointment to give us an update on how well he is doing. She keeps telling me how appreciative she is that you are cooking for him. "

"Have you heard anything from you new lawyer?" asked Sophie.

"Shh." Lydia looked around and whispered behind her hands, "These walls have ears and those are real cameras you see everywhere." She sat down on the cot and started to cough. Sophie sat down and started patting her on the back and the others gathered around her as if they were concerned with the coughing spell. She pretended to clear her throat as she continued to talk behind her hand, "Even though things are getting better here, I have learned not to trust anyone. When I talked with Samuel he told me not to let it be known that I am looking into getting another lawyer. He called it not showing our hand. He also told me to get a transcript of the hearing. You should have heard Felix Fields squawk when I insisted that I needed to go over the evidence myself. He accused me of everything in the book. Of course some of it is true. I am going behind his back by getting another lawyer, which I haven't told him yet because nothing is final." With a final cough Lydia raised her head and the conversation continued in a normal tone.

Feeling that the topic was safe enough Sophie asked about the trial date. "I haven't heard yet. But my lawyer Felix Fields said that he was working on it .He still thinks that my best bet is to me to plea bargain. He keeps saying that I probably had partial amnesia. It doesn't seem to get it through his thick head that not remembering while you are unconscious isn't amnesia."

"I'm sorry ladies. I gave you extra time. But my job may be on the line if I let you stay too long." The guard opened the door to escort them out.

As they said their goodbyes Lydia gave them Samuel's number and casually mentioned that they might want to call her friend Kate to let her know that things were getting better. They got the message that she was sending, 'communication between Lydia and Samuel is to be channeled through Sophie'. Samuel might fill them in on what was happening at that end.

Before Samuel contacted Jim Osborne, the lawyer his friend had recommended He checked Mr. Osborne's legal record and background. He found that he was the best lawyer around and highly respected in his field. He was known for his tact and diplomacy but could be as hard as nails when it came to protecting and representing his client. He did not always take on a case just because a friend asked him to. He was so much in demand that he could choose the cases he wanted. He would not take a client if he felt that he did not have the time do it justice. So there were times when he had to turn down a client but he tried to find another lawyer that would help in his stead. Samuel was impressed and when he discussed this with Kate they both decided that he had to be Lydia's lawyer.

Samuel called and set up an appointment to meet with Mr. Osborne. He explained that Lydia, a childhood friend of his wife Kate had been charged with murder. Samuel told Mr. Osborne that the trial would be in Windfield several states away. Mr. Osborne explained that he had a heavy case load and that he would have to check to see if he would have time to take on a client that far away. He took his work seriously and always wanted to give a client his best. The next day Samuel and Kate met Mr. Osborne for lunch to find out what he had decided about taking Lydia's case. He had made up his mind to decline because of the travel distance. But Kate was such a great advocate for her best friend she persuaded him to change his mind. Samuel had also thrown in a voucher for his travel as an incentive.

As soon as Sophie returned home from visiting Lydia in jail she called Kate. "Sophie, I am so glad that you called." Samuel and I are planning on visiting soon. Is there any way you can find out if Lydia's house is still closed as a crime scene? Mr. Osborn thought it might be a good idea if we stay there. That would give him easy access to the house so he can check out the scene without anyone asking questions."

"Yes I think it should okay for you to stay at Lydia's. I took your suitcases there from the hotel after you left in such a hurry .I put them in the spare bedroom. I'll tell Lydia tomorrow that you will be visiting soon. I know she'll be glad to see you." She told Kate that Lydia was doing better now that she had something to occupy her mind. They had a long conversation about all that had been going on since she left. Kate told Sophie that Samuel wanted her to keep her ears open to anything that will help Lydia. "I've been checking the Windfield news on line but there's nothing like the grapevine. There's usually a little truth in gossip. We just have to weed out the embellishments."

Jim Osborn was in a conference room where there were papers in different stacks on a long table. In one area were the news clippings that Kate had sent him. The transcript of the trial was in another. Several open law books were off to the side on another table. He had made a list of the people who would be called to testify. He had gone over them all. "I need to get down to Windfield and have a face to face meeting with each one. It doesn't seem that Mr. Fields has done his homework, but I don't want to get on the bad side of the local lawyer." He stood up and stretched his back, "Here's where the fun begins."

He made a quick call to Sophie in Whitfield. He had a list of things he wanted her to do. He wanted her to let Mr. Fields know that he will be helping in Lydia's defense. "I don't want to antagonize him that's why we will just tell him that I will be there to help. Tell Lydia to explain this to Mr. Fields. Then Lydia needs to let the district attorney know that I will be called in as an additional attorney. That way Lydia will have the right to place a call to me if she needs to. Have her call me as soon as she contacts these people. There's one more thing I want you do. Go to the insurance office there and see if they can tell you how to get in touch with Mr. Williams."

Since the forensic team had finished gathering evidence at Lydia's house her friends were allowed to stay there as long as things were left things in the same place. This of course was what they had intended to do. Jim Osborn stayed at the hotel and visited the Martin house often to confer with Kate and Samuel. After a lengthy discussion with the judge and district attorney, Jim was successful in getting the judge to let Lydia out on bail. However the bail was very high and Lydia was on house arrest. She had to wear an ankle bracelet with electronic monitoring. But it felt good to be back in her own house even for a short spell.

After getting Lydia settled in her house, Jim, Lydia, Kate and Sammy started to sort through the evidence that had been brought out during the pre-trials. They talked with the witnesses and each one could not offer anything new. Most of the witnesses were very apologetic and hated that what they knew would hurt Lydia's case. It didn't look good for Lydia. Even though the evidence was circumstantial there were too many coincidences that pointed to Lydia.

Mr. Fields was highly insulted that a big shot lawyer from Minnesota was called in. But after Jim Osborne talked with him, he agreed to be part of the defense team. He knew that this trial was something big in Windfield and he wanted to be in on it even though he thought Lydia might be guilty. He continued to say that Lydia's best chance was to plead guilty but under extenuating circumstances. He said that the very testimony that the prosecuting attorney used against her could very well be testimony in her favor. The main ones were from the preacher who all but threw her out of the church and the two scenes at Denny's where Lydia was so upset at Leroy and Leroy's hot temper. Then there was the fact that Lydia couldn't remember, which to Felix was a psychological trauma called partial amnesia. He also recalled the visit by the psychologist that Lydia forgot to tell him about. He still refused to believe that Lydia thought he was just an annoying guest of Leroy's. All this could have caused Lydia to snap.

Jim suggested that Felix could be doing some leg work since his business was slow. Felix, who didn't want this big town lawyer to think he was a nobody in a small town, so he suddenly found that he had a heavy caseload. This played right into Jim's hands. This would keep him busy while the team continued to search for clues. After going over and over the evidence and finding nothing new, Felix's suggestion that Lydia go for a plea bargain began to look attractive.

Chapter 25

It was such a gloomy day when the trial began it seemed that the whole world was mourning for Lydia. Things did not look at all favorable in her case. The defense team had gone over every detail. They were praying for some break. If nothing came forward it looked more and more like Lydia would spend many years in jail. The jury process took most of the morning. After charging the jury the judge called a recess for lunch. After lunch the jury was addressed by both the prosecution and the defense. As each witness was called there was nothing to dispute. About all the defense had was the good character of Lydia and the fact that she was also injured, injured so badly that she spent 2 weeks in a coma.

The next day the prosecution called each witness to the stand. The paramedics were called first. They reported that there were several women and a man there. They described the condition of Leroy and Lydia. They found Lydia unconscious on the sofa and Leroy on the floor near the glider. Lydia had a gash on her forehead. Leroy who had a big gash in the back of the head was dead. When the sheriff and deputy arrived they were in the process of placing Lydia on a stretcher to transport her to the hospital. They left Leroy's body there to be transported after the forensic team had finished. The coroner reported that Leroy died from a blow to the back of the skull. The sheriff also testified. He described the scene inside the house. He also described the process that he went through trying to trace down each possible lead. He explained that his best lead was a thief who was later found to be in another county at the time. He also went on to discount Mr. Williams the insurance salesman who found them. Molly was called to the stand to describe the evening that Lydia came in all upset. This took a long time because Molly an unwilling witness did not elaborate. The prosecution attorney had to prompt her with questions. The forensics expert described the scene and reported the different places where blood was found. He reported that a brass lamp, which was placed into evidence and marked as the murder weapon. It had blood on it but had been wiped off. When Reverend Goodman was called, he described Lydia's unusual behavior just as he had before. To back up his testimony Dr. Jonas Meuller was called testify that he, a psychologist found Lydia in an unstable state. Lydia was still angry at the fact that he came to her house and interviewed her without her consent and asked questions that were too personal. She had thought he was a nosy friend of Leroy's. Lydia's lawyer Jim Osborne objected to his testimony because she had not known she was being interviewed. The judge agreed to take it into consideration and it may be stricken later. The most damaging evidence came from Mr. Agnew who read the accident double indemnity clause in the insurance policy that Leroy had just taken out on himself. The sheriff was then recalled to the stand. He explained about the plane ticket to Missouri for the week of the accident and the packed luggage. The attorney commented that Lydia must not have planned on the knock on the head causing a coma. The defense immediately called an objection. The judge reprimanded the prosecution attorney and warned that that kind of comments would not be tolerated in his courtroom.

Felix still insisted that it would be in Lydia's best interest to not take the stand. Things were looking so bad the defense team started seriously considering a plea bargain. Jim Osborne felt that she may plead temporary insanity and probably get less jail time than if the trial continued. Lydia would not hear of it she said she would trust God and the jury. If she was found guilty she would just have to accept it.

Phillip Williams entered his insurance office in Chicago and looked around as he took off his coat and set his briefcase on his desk. Everything was the same as he had left it but I didn't appear the same to him. Since his sister's accident he had changed. Everyday things seemed to be more important. For the first time in a long time he realized how precious life was. He realized that family was so much more important than work. He vowed to take more time with his family. He would take a vacation with his loving and patient wife Teresa and their two precious children. He may even do what his sister Julie did. He could buy a camper and go camping like his family did when he was growing up. He remembered the good times they had just being together and enjoying the historical sites of the United States. He had learned a lot from traveling around. Some of the simplest things were the most memorable. He could almost smell the bacon frying on the Coleman camp stove they always carried.

His reminiscing was interrupted as Sally, his secretary, handed him a fistful of notes from people who had called while he was gone. "Mr. Williams it is so good to have you back. By the way, how's Julie?" Phillip had returned from Iowa where his sister, Julie, was hospitalized. She was recovering from a serious accident.

"She's on the mend but her doctor wants her to stay in Iowa a week longer to see how the therapy is working. It is going to be a long healing process but I think she will be fine. It has been such a strain on Mom and me seeing just how bad the accident was. She is so lucky to be alive. God must have been with her that day."

"I am so glad that she is going to be all right. Welcome back. Your desk is covered with work waiting for your return. Doesn't that make you feel wanted?" Sally teased. "I think the first order of business is back in Windfield though. Mr. Agnew is on the line and refuses to hang up until he speaks with you. He has been calling every day since you were gone. I can't put him off any longer. Since you left orders not to transfer calls to your cell phone I have been fending him off for you. But he said that he would come up here in person if he had to."

"Williams here," Phillip spoke into the phone. How are things in Windfield?"

"Not good at all. You sold a policy to a Leroy Martin who died."

"I know he died. I am the one who found the Martins. I hated to leave in such a hurry but there was an emergency here at the main office. How is Mrs. Martin?"

"Not good. That's the problem she has been charged with Leroy's murder."

"What? Leroy murdered? Why in the world would Lydia be charged? She was unconscious when I found her."

"They haven't found anyone else who was at the house at that time and the double indemnity clause in the policy you sold him didn't help. That's just one of the reasons for charging her. Just so you know they checked you out too. They came to this office and checked your phone records against the time Leroy was killed and found that you were here when he died. Your call to the airport and the time you left this office was enough to let you off the hook. The sheriff did want to talk with you but he didn't think there was any cause to bother you since there were others who arrived after you called them. Now I need to know how to handle this claim."

"Just sit tight until I get back with you." He hung up the phone and called to his secretary. "Sally, go on line and get me everything you can find on a Martin murder trial in Windfield."

Phillip dialed the sheriff's office in Windfield.

"Sheriff's office," Cliff answered when Phillip called.

"I need to speak with the sheriff."

"He's not here. He and Deputy Crane are at the courthouse."

"To whom am I speaking?"

"I'm Cliff. I work for the sheriff whenever he needs extra help. Today I'm just answering the phone. Is there anything I can do for you? I can't call the sheriff on his cell because he has it cut off."

"Cliff, this is Phillip Williams. Maybe you remember that I used be an insurance agent there."

"Oh yeah, I remember you. You were the first one on the murder scene at the Martin house. I heard the sheriff say he tried to get in touch with you but you had an emergency in the family. My friend Bessie told me that you were leaving when she and her friends got there. Bessie and I have been friends for awhile. We usually get together to watch football games at her house during the season. But she always invites the other 4 other cohorts from church. She and her friends can't get over that bloody scene. We can't even enjoy a simple football game for all the yakking. Did you know that Lydia did it?"

Phillip was startled and started to end the call and tell Cliff that he would call back later, but Cliff seemed to be in a talkative mood. "*This conversation is getting interesting,*" He thought. "No I didn't know that. Has she been found guilty?"

"No but she is being tried right now. That's where the sheriff and deputy Crane are now. At first they wouldn't let her out on bail because they thought she might run. Then her new lawyer came and talked the judge into releasing her on bond."

Phillip didn't know what he was talking about but he let him continue talking. "How is Mrs. Martin? She must be a frantic with her husband dead and then being thrown in jail for his murder on top of that."

"Well, yes I heard she was a wreck walking back and forth until she got that job cooking for Mr. Carter.

"I'm sure this whole thing is taking a toll on her. It's good that she had something occupy her mind until the trial came up. "

"Yes it was very hard on her. She seems to be doing better now that she has another lawyer. I heard that the new lawyer, Mr. Osborne, came to help her other lawyer. Mr. Fields was fit to be tied when Lydia told him about it. He was visiting her here at the jail and as he left I was about to ask when the trial would begin. But he stormed past me saying, "I don't need some big time lawyer from Minnesota coming here to help me out."

He was still on the phone with Cliff when Sally knocked and stuck her head inside the door. Phillip put his hand over the mouth piece, "Yes, Sally."

"It's the Mr. Agnew from field office in Windfield again."

"Cliff, I'm sorry, something just came up. I have to hang up. It's been good talking with you. Tell the sheriff I'll call later."

"Mr. Williams I took the message. Sophie Pearson was just in Mr. Agnew's office. She said that Lydia has a lawyer from Minnesota who will be helping Mr. Fields in her case. Anyway her lawyer Jim Osborne wants to speak with you. Here's his office number."

Phillip and Jim had a long conversation about the Martin incident. Phillip also suggested that Jim call the sheriff's office and talk with Cliff if he was still there. "I just got off the phone with him and he likes to talk. He may be a well of information. It seems that he is friends with the Church Committee. They were the women who came with the preacher to the house that day I found that terrible scene at the Martin's."

There was very little that Phillip could tell Jim about the incident. He was there such a short time. All he could tell him was that he had an appointment with Leroy. It seemed that Leroy had a concern that could not wait. Leroy insisted that Phillip come that day. Even though Phillip told him that he had urgent business in Chicago he was persistent. "I tried to get him to wait a few days until my replacement came but he would not hear of it. I didn't have very much time to get to the Martin house and the airport. But I hurried out there on my way to the airport. There's not much to tell." He went on to tell Mr. Osborne how he knocked many times but no one answered. Leroy had told him that sometimes he was out back working. But searching around the house he found no one. The car and truck were there indicating that the Martins were home. Since Leroy had been so insistent about the matter, Phillip opened the door and found them on the floor. That's when he called 911 and then the preacher. Since he was new to Windfield he didn't know many people there, the preacher was the only one he thought to call. Then he left the situation in the hands of Preacher Goodman and the 5 members of the church committee. That was all Phillip could think of to tell Jim about that fateful day.

After he ended the call, Jim wondered why Leroy was so adamant about Phillip coming immediately. Did it have something with the existing insurance policy? Did he want to change it? What happened between the time he took it out and that day? When he thought about the events leading up to that day, there were pieces of the puzzle that didn't fit. Was there a big storm brewing between Lydia and Leroy? Did she really do it? Maybe Felix was right maybe she did need to plea bargain. Kate and Samuel were positive that Lydia was innocent. But were they too close to see the whole picture?

The next day Jim met with Lydia before the trial began. He told her about the conversation with Phillip. Since Lydia was unconscious she knew nothing about Phillip's visit. She told Jim that she didn't even know that Leroy had asked him to come by. This was not unusual she said because Leroy hardly ever told her about what he did. Jim had asked Kate and Samuel to join them in the conference room. He hated to tell them the bad news but it seemed that there was nothing else he could do. When he told them that he wanted to ask for a plea bargain, Lydia and Kate both gasped fear showed in both their faces. "You can't mean it," Kate choked back a tear. "Lydia is incapable of murder." Lydia was so shocked she could not speak. After recounting the evidence against Lydia that had been brought out in the trial, Jim convinced Samuel that her best option would be to accept a bargain.

When Kate insisted that there would be no way that Lydia would plead guilty under any circumstances, Jim reminded her of the letter. "The letter you wrote to Lydia begging her to visit is already in evidence. In the letter you yourself talked about how different she sounded. That was the reason for the plane ticket. You were worried about her state of mind. You have to admit that that does not help in her defense. It is just one more thing the prosecution can use against her.

So it was decided. The district attorney would be called first thing in the morning to discuss their options. There was a group of friends at Lydia's that evening to console her. They wanted to show their support. Kate and Samuel were still staying there. The two attorneys were also present. Food had been brought in but no one felt like eating. The conversation was at a minimum. No one wanted to discuss what might happen to Lydia. "I wonder who could be coming at this late hour," someone said as headlights were seen coming down the farm driveway.

"I just couldn't get Lydia off my mend," Phillip said as he stepped out of the rental car. "I caught a late flight out to see if there was something I could do. I have been keeping up with the trial on the internet." After introductions were made, Jim and Phillip were standing in the hallway talking. "Lydia is such gentle soul I can't believe she could have killed her husband even if he was a pompous braggart. He looked around and saw that Lydia was out of ear shot. He didn't want to upset her even more with his thoughts of her departed husband. "Right here is where I last saw Lydia before today," he said as he pointed down at the floor. "It has been a long day." He looked around and found that the only seat available was an ugly pink glider. "**Whoa here!**" he yelled when he sat down.

The next morning instead of meeting with the District attorney, Jim asked the judge for a continuance of two days. "Since you assured me that there is new evidence that is germane to this case, I will grant the two days. But let me be very clear it had better be substantial. Court is adjourned and will convene in two days." The judge rapped the gavel and left the bench.

The next two days held a flurry of activity at the Martin house.

Chapter 26

THE TWO DAYS CONTINUANCE HAD passed, the courtroom was packed. The air was filled with expectation. This was Lydia's last chance to go for a lesser sentence. If she was going to ask for a plea bargain she would have to do it now.

Lawyer Jim Osborne recalled Bessie to the stand, "Bessie I want you to tell the jury again what happened when you went to the Martin house on June 28th."

The District attorney stood to her feet, "Objection Your Honor this isn't new. This witness has already told the court what she knows." She turned to Jim, "Mr. Osborne why are you wasting the taxpayer's money extending this trial?"

"A woman's life is at stake here. Isn't her life a few minutes of the court's time?" retorted Jim back at her.

"Will both attorneys approach the bench?" The judge warned both to control themselves. He reminded Mr. Osborne of his warning that he must show new evidence. Jim assured that he would get to it but this questioning was important.

When he returned to the table he again questioned Bessie. He asked her to close her eyes so as to have no distraction. "Now Bessie we're going try to take this a step at a time. Try not to look at the whole picture at once. I you to take each step as I direct you. You are walking in the door, what is the first thing you see?"

"Blood, oh my, oh my, blood, blood everywhere."

"Yes, I know Bessie," Jim spoke in a calm quiet voice. "Just keep your eyes closed. Where is Leroy?"

"On the floor with his chair on him," she slowly answered as if she was trying to get it right. Jim assured her that she was doing fine. The he asked where Lydia was.

"Essie and I were trying to get her to stay on the sofa but she kept sliding off. Cindy Lou tried to clean the blood off Poor Lydia's head." She opened her eyes and looked at Lydia, "I'm so sorry Lydia. I was trying to help you."

"Close your eyes again Bessie, so you can focus on that scene." Jim instructed her and asked again. "Where was Lydia when you found her? Was she on the floor or on the couch or somewhere else?"

"Leading the witness," Was the objection.

"Okay, I'll repeat the question. Focus, you say you tried to keep her on the couch. Was she on the couch when you first saw her?"

Bessie's eyes popped open in surprise, "Oh my goodness. Now I remember. No, she wasn't near the sofa. She was in the hall, Essie and I had a time getting her to the sofa. With the blood all over I forgot about that."

"Just a small technicality, it doesn't change the evidence that much," came the remark from the prosecution"

The coroner was called again to the stand. When he was asked about Leroy's height his answer was six feet 3 inches. Then Jim asked if he had known Leroy's mother. His answer was affirmative. "Do you think Leroy got his height from his mother?" he was asked. "Heavens no," was the answer. "She was short, about five feet."

"That's all I wanted to know. Thank you."

Jim nodded to Samuel who went out and returned with the pink glider. With this the spectators sat up with anticipation. Next a woman walked in with a life-like doll. "How tall are you?" asked Jim. "Five feet was the answer." Jim asked her to pretend she was Leroy's mother who rocked him in the rocker. She did so and then was excused. Those in the audience sat back with the look of disappointment.

The Jim turned to the judge, "With the court's permission, I would like to try to re-create the scene of the crime. Now I will set up the room as it was at the Martin house that day. Please be patient as we set the scene. Several walls were wheeled in. On them were drawings of the tools from the walls of the Martin house. Then some of the other items from the house were brought in which included the recliner, a table, a brass lamp, which had been identified as the murder weapon, an anvil, which was so heavy that a hoist brought it in, and some farm tools.

Jim recalled the sheriff to the stand, "Let me recall some facts that you told the court. Jim turned pages and then read from them. Lydia told you about Leroy's routine when he came in from the fields. You commented that Lydia laughed because she thought it was funny that he used the pink glider take his steel toed boots off, then moved over to sit in his recliner. She also said that Leroy had trouble taking his boots off because they were too small. Is this so?" The sheriff answered, "Yes," and was excused.

Everyone sat on the edge of their seats when a high cage made of reinforced steel was wheeled in. It was placed around the scene.

A hush came over the entire courtroom as a tall man walked in. He was wearing a crash helmet with thick padding on the back. His steel toed boots clicked on the wooden floor as he walked. He entered the cage and sat down in the pink glider. He lifted a foot, untied the strings of the boot and tugged at it. It was so snug that it did not budge so the man tugged harder. The boot shot into the air slamming onto the cage as the pink glider flipped over. The man's head crashed onto the anvil which made a huge dent in the pliable plastic on the back of the helmet.

Epilogue

Lydia was content. She smiled as she looked out over the landscape. So much had changed in the two years since the trial. She did love the wide open spaces of the farm. She had built her "Dream House" and the "starter house" was now was a guest house which was used often. Her clients kept her busy designing home interiors. She especially loved designing the mechanical modern conveniences. The big barn Leroy insisted he needed was converted into a business office. The outside walls now were mostly glass and looked out over the spacious lawn. Beyond that was the beautiful brook that she had fallen in love with when they moved there. Flowering shrubbery surrounded the converted barn and a winding path led to the brook. Sammy and Melissa's horses grazed in several paddocks that were on the other side of the brook. They now rented the rest of the farm where they raised quarter horses. Children from the Shiphrah House were invited to come out anytime to ride.

She still had loss of memory of that fateful day. But a little voice comes to her sometimes, "He was making fun of you again but did you really have to push him that hard?"

REFERENCE

SC R Holland Doris
Holland Doris
Dangerous occupation

ACL-MAIN
27894047

NO LONGER PROPERTY OF ANDERSON COUNTY LIBRARY